ENGINES
OF THE
BROKEN
WORLD

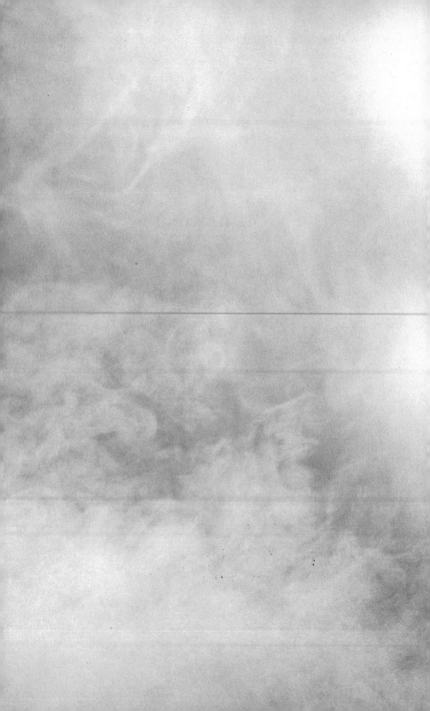

ENGINES
OF THE
BROKEN
WORLD

JASON VANHEE

HENRY HOLT AND COMPANY

NEW YORK

Henry Holt and Company, LLC
Publishers since 1866
175 Fifth Avenue
New York, New York 10010
macteenbooks.com

Library of Congress Cataloging-in-Publication Data
Vanhee, Jason.
Engines of the broken world / Jason Vanhee.
pages   cm
Summary: In a rural village far distant from the dead and dying cities,
twelve-year-old Merciful discovers horrible secrets and must make decisions
that may save or doom her world.
ISBN 978-0-8050-9629-3 (hardcover)
[1. Supernatural—Fiction.   2. Science fiction.]   I. Title.
PZ7.V4En 2013   [Fic]—dc23   2013026768

Henry Holt books may be purchased for business or promotional use.
For information on bulk purchases, please contact the Macmillan Corporate
and Premium Sales Department at (800) 221-7945 x5442
or by e-mail at specialmarkets@macmillan.com.

First Edition—2013

Printed in the United States of America / Designed by April Ward

1 3 5 7 9 10 8 6 4 2

To Adam.

It's true this book would exist without you,
but no one would ever have read it.
That's not much of an existence. Thank you
for giving one to this book. And to me.

So when this world's compounded union breaks,
Time ends and to old Chaos all things turn;
Confused stars shall meet, celestial fire
Fleet on the floods, the earth shoulder the sea,
Affording it no shore, and Phoebe's wain
Chase Phoebus and enraged affect his place,
And strive to shine by day, and full of strife
Dissolve the engines of the broken world.

—Lucan, Pharsalia
Translated by Christopher Marlowe

ONE

It snowed the day our mother died, snow so hard and so soft at the same time that we could neither bury her nor take her out to the barn. So we set her, my brother and me, under the table in the kitchen, and we left her there because we didn't know what else to do. There wasn't anyone else to ask, our father dead for years and the village nearly empty and no one to help out two kids left alone in the winter.

Except it wasn't winter, not really. It was October. Storm like that, with snow like that, we shouldn't have had till much later, till Christmastime, or even past that more like. But we didn't spend much time thinking about how the weather had gotten all strange. We just dealt with it.

The Minister wasn't happy, but then, it wasn't happy with much of anything these days. There wasn't much holy going on, and we didn't pray like we used to, or give it milk to lap up like in golden summertime. The cow had run dry before it died, and the goats were as skinny as fence posts and dried up just like the cow. We didn't have treats for the little thing the way we would've in happier times. But still it yowled and protested when we decided to move Mama away from her bed and put her in the kitchen, which was almost as cold as outdoors, because that wasn't the way.

"She that bred and birthed you both, and you set her in the cold like that," the Minister said. It was an old model, a worn-down thing that couldn't do much more than cavil and complain at us and hadn't done much more than that, to be truthful, since we were born. My brother just ignored the beast, like he always did, but he was halfway to the Devil, even our mama had said so, and there was nothing more to be done. For me, I felt bad when the little thing hissed its words at us, and didn't know what all to do about it. Ministers were the word of rightness, and it hurt to not do what it said, but my brother, he had the way of it when he made his suggestion, and I couldn't disagree with him.

"We got to move her, Merciful," he said, and I just looked up from crying, because it was a daughter's job to weep even if you didn't feel it at all.

"Move her where? It's cold as sin. We can't go out."

He allowed that, and nodded his head even, as if *he* felt we couldn't, which I didn't believe one bit. My brother would've mumbled half of a prayer and dragged Mama out himself, if he thought there was a point. With the Minister right there on the coverlet letting itself be seen, though, he knew that he had to do something a little more right than wrong, and that was let himself be led just a bit by his sister.

"Not outside, I guess you're right. But she'll go sour here."

I didn't say yes, but then, I didn't say no, and when he took her body under the arms and gestured me to her feet, I took them up and helped him. The Minister paced around our legs with its tail whipping back and forth and said it wasn't right at all. The kitchen was chill like it never should be, but we hadn't had a cooked meal in days, since Mama took sick, and most all our wood had gone to the hearth in her room, instead of for stew or bread or what have you. So we laid her out there, under the table, and the Minister padded around her and shook its head at us, and we left her in the dark.

We went back into the bedroom, which was as far from the kitchen as we could get and the warmest place besides. The big bed and our little kids' beds that slid out of a cupboard were all tidied up, and on the shelf the books that my mother had read to me when I was young were in just the right place, and so were all the clothes and everything else. Except for the bed, where the dent of her body was still warm and the pillow still showed where she had been. The Minister had come with us— always came with us now because there wasn't hardly anyone else for it to attend to—and settled into the room's one chair, the rocker that rested in the corner near the hearth. It stared at us with its yellow eyes. The Minister didn't say anything, but you could almost feel what it was thinking and tell that it didn't think the best of us, two ungrateful children. And I turned away from its stare, because I *was* ungrateful, and didn't regret it, and didn't want to do anything to make it better.

What Gospel felt I didn't know. He and I hadn't ever been close since I was still small enough to suck my thumb and make dolls from sticks. He'd been a wild thing even then, barely wanting to talk to us, barely heeding the Minister, barely sleeping inside the house save when, as now, the weather turned hard and brutal outside or there were things wilder than him around. But I remembered that, when I was very small, he used to talk to me sometimes and tell me things about trees or birds, or about the beasts that slunk by in the darkness and made a meal of anyone so uncautious as to be seen, which Gospel never was. We lost neighbors that way, their houses gaping empty without a body inside, but sometimes there'd be blood spilled on porches or a window broke right out and curtains torn. Gospel knew all the secrets of the beasts and knew how to keep from them. When I was young he tried to teach me, lessons taught in a tongue I couldn't quite grasp, until about the time Papa died he gave up in frustration and we never much talked after.

Now Gospel was sitting on his little truckle bed, the

one his legs barely fit on any longer. His big feet hung over, with his shoulders leaning against my bed half-pulled out from the wall where he sat. His hair was dark and wild, filthy with grease and held back, as much as it was, with a tie of leather from a big cat, one of the things almost safe to hunt, though not to eat. His hands were scarred and dirty, the nails torn where he held them before his mouth, staring blindly out, maybe at the Minister, who stared right back, but maybe not, maybe at the fire instead. Gospel was almost fifteen, near three years older than me, a man or close enough, though there was no one left to say if he was or wasn't. He was, in fact, The Man, the only one we knew of, though there were still two other women, so I wasn't The anything. At his belt he had a big knife, with a ragged leather-wrapped hilt, and a gun that didn't have any bullets but that he wouldn't let away from himself for any dear thing at all. That gun had been Papa's, and I remembered the sound it made the last time it was ever fired, when Papa got himself killed by a stranger in a fight six years ago. Gospel's held it close ever since, for what earthly reason I could never imagine.

He noticed me scrutinizing him, and he shot me a look fierce as the cold wind outside, and then he turned away all at once because the Minister gave a little hiss. Gospel was my brother. He wasn't supposed to hate me, but I thought sometimes he did, and I think the Minister thought it too.

"You're each all the other has left," the Minister said, soft as snow falling against a paper window, barely in hearing above the crackle and pop of the burning wood.

"Don't think I don't know that," Gospel said with fire in his voice, almost settled but not quite yet, still a boy mixed with a man.

"There's knowing, and then there is knowing," the Minister replied, and curled its tail up and around to wiggle in the air, with that attitude that it got sometimes to make me want to pull out all its whiskers.

"I know it too well, Minister."

The Minister only hummed a considering hum and turned to look at me, where I was trying to barely see it out of the corner of my eye, and none too successful at being sneaky like that. "Merciful, do you know as well as your brother?"

"I know. I know he's all I got, and all I'll ever have, like as not, the way the world's going."

"The world goes as it's meant," the Minister said, like it always did if you asked it a question about such things. Furious it could make me, and was coming close now, though it could be kind as well, and it would be, I was sure, once we asked it nicely to do so. It was made to look after us, body and soul, and it would if it could, though what exactly a thing in the shape of a fat gray cat could do to protect our bodies I'd never been sure.

"So it was meant for Mama to die tonight?"

The Minister tilted its head to the side and stared at

me. "I suppose you could say it must have been, or else she couldn't have done so."

"Don't even talk to it, Merciful. It didn't help with Mama all these years; it's not going to help us now."

"You don't know, Gospel. Maybe it knows things."

"Like what? What do you think it knows?"

"Secret things," I said, and the Minister hummed and repeated me.

"Secret things," it said in a sort of hissing whisper. "I know many secrets, yes."

"Tell me one thing you know that I don't!" Gospel demanded, springing to his feet. He stepped around the tail end of the big bed, toward the chair. I stood in the doorway still and didn't dare to move.

"I know the beginning and end of all things," the Minister said.

"So you knew our mother was going to die?"

"Everything dies, Gospel."

My brother shook his shaggy head and turned to me. "Soon as the snow stops, soon as the weather turns again, I'm gone, Merciful. I stayed for her," he said, gesturing past me to the darkness behind, "but she don't need me anymore. You can come or not, I don't mind either way, but if you come, I won't slow down for you."

"You can't leave me," I said.

"You'll be leaving yourself, if you want to stay. Anyway, the darned Minister here will help you through it all, just like it helped Mama." His voice was all sarcasm and bitterness, but then he shook his head again and sighed. "Don't matter yet, anyhow. The weather's going to be like this for a spell, I suppose."

"A long spell, indeed," the Minister said. Gospel gave it a hard look; but then, he had a supply of those laid up to give to the thing. It paid him no mind and then curled up on the chair and seemed to fall asleep—not that I believed it, and neither did Gospel, I'm sure.

We didn't say anything for a time, Gospel still standing at the foot of the bed, almost so close that I could've reached out and touched him, but so far away that I couldn't even connect. Then he growled a little and pushed past me into the dark, and a minute later light flared up as I turned slowly around, and there he was, plopped down on the bigger of the two chairs in the sitting room, with the empty doorway to the kitchen framing him from behind and an oil lamp on the table beside him. He didn't say anything, but he pointed with his first two right-hand fingers at the other chair, our mother's chair, which was just next to the table. I nodded and went to sit in the little pool of light.

It was silent in that room, with the two chairs in the middle of the chamber; a loom up against the back wall; a chest with spare clothes; and a box that held old wooden toys, most of them carved by Gospel for himself and then given to me when he got too old to bother with them. Not by Gospel; Mama gave them to me in the narrow space when she still cared a bit about the world after he had already quit. There was the big old bearskin rug in front of the chairs where I would sit and do my lessons or knit or whatever it was that I did in all those days that had gone by. Papa got that rug by shooting a bear back when there were still bullets for the rifle, grown rusty and pointless, that hung beside the door. There wasn't a sound except for a faint pop now and again, and the fainter hiss of snow on the roof, and once, perilous quiet, the sound of a cat yawning.

"So are you coming with me?"

"I don't know any woodcraft," I said.

"You'll learn. Or you won't, I guess. But there's nothing here anymore, Merce. Nothing to stay for, no one at all. There's other places, there's got to be," he said, sounding maybe a little desperate, maybe a little defiant. "Places where there are people still. I can find you one and leave you there, and then I can head out on my own and not fret."

"You wouldn't fret about me, Gospel," I said, with more venom than I thought I had in me.

He lowered his face so that the tangles of his dark hair fell over it. "Maybe I wouldn't. But maybe today I feel like I should, and I'm going to for a bit. How's that? Go through the motions for you, if you like that better. The point is, I'll take you away if you come as soon as we can go, and I'll get you someplace with more people, someplace you can make a life in, not this dead little pit of a village."

I leaned forward and brushed away his hair, so that he looked up through his thick eyelashes at me. "I don't know anyplace else, Gospel. How can I live anywhere but here?"

"How can you live *here*? There's nothing left. Two goats and four chickens, Widow Cally through the orchard that hardly produces, and Jenny Gone way up the other side of Stony Mountain. The Minister? That's it, Merciful, that's all you have here. The Widow's past seventy, and Jenny's half as crazy as Mama was, and that's still saying a lot. You got to come away with me, or you'll die."

"I'll die out there anyways. There's nobody left out there, either, Gospel. When was the last time a tinker came by? When I was six. I remember because Mama bought me two ribbons for my hair for my seventh birthday. Six years, Gospel, since we've seen anyone, unless you've seen somebody and never told."

He lifted his head and swallowed. There was dark fuzz on his upper lip, the mustache he had tried to grow in for months but it never yet came, and it made him look like what he was, a boy trying too hard to be The Man. "I see signs sometimes. Footprints, an old coat in good shape hanging on a stump like somebody just took it off a day before, and once I saw a snare. But no people, no. Nothing like that."

"So what do you think we can find, Gospel?"

"Something. Anything. There's got to be someone left. We can't be all there is."

And I knew then that for all he played the part of the outsider, he was the one who needed this place, who needed Mama and me, more than I had ever needed him.

"How far have you gone, Gospel?"

"Oh, Lord. Days down the river, and two days up it till it's just a trickle in the rocks, and over Windblown Ridge, and down past the Hollows. I've gone everyplace I could think to go, Merciful, and I've seen places where people were once, empty houses and broken roads and graves dug deep back in the forest where nothing could disturb them. Never a soul, though. But they got to be out there, right?" He smiled, a little hopefully, at me, his sister who he hated maybe but needed for certain, and I didn't have it in me to hate him right then, so I reached out and took hold of his hand.

"I bet the Widow Cally has a map up at her place, and we can look and see where you've been, and see where you could go to maybe find somebody. And if you did, we could all go, the four of us, and we could live with them." Or they could come live with us, but I didn't say that, even though I didn't ever want to go from home.

"Do you think she does? I never had the courage to ask."

"Well, you're the head of the house now, Gospel. Neighbor to neighbor, you can ask her anything."

He nodded slightly. "Yeah, I suppose I can, can't I? I suppose I can walk right on up there and ask if she's got a map, and by the way, our mother's dead."

It got real quiet again after he said that, both of us thinking of the thin, sad woman who was growing cold in the kitchen, and all the snow falling so we couldn't bury her, and how terrible it was to be orphans in the end of the world.

Two

THE DARK WAS WELL SETTLED OUTSIDE, AND THE NIGHT far along, when I finally thought to get to sleep. There were things that needed doing, and Gospel, for Heaven's sake, wasn't going to do them, nor the Minister obviously, so it was just me.

I had to look through Mama's things to see what was of value and what of use and what of sentiment, and keep them and then dispose of the rest. A few things might suit for the Widow, or for Jenny Gone on her mountain, and those I set aside. And then there were things that would never do for anyone, old clothes that I had never really seen that were too big for me and probably always would be: for Mama was tall, and I didn't seem likely to sprout like a vine. Them I had to start to take apart, and set in the chests by the loom, for scraps and for material. And since I was doing that, and since he was here, I set to mending Gospel's cloak, which was rather tattered, and his jacket, which was worn out at the elbows, and his spare pants, which had raggedy hems and patches of furry skin sewn over the knees. He sat and watched at first, my stitches more clever than his ever were (though he thought himself skilled with a needle), and then after a time he left me in Mama's chair in the sitting room and went into the bedroom, where the light was grown dim because the fire was almost gone, and I supposed he went to bed.

I was just finishing up on his trousers, which could have used a washing and were thin as onion skin on the seat—about which I wasn't sure what to do—when the Minister came padding out of the bedroom and settled on the rug, staring up at me. The creature came and went as it pleased, most often here, but sometimes, we gathered, up to the Widow Cally's. If it ever went so far as Jenny Gone's, we didn't hear of it, but then, we didn't hear much of Jenny at all, her being three hours' walk away, and Gospel having already learned all he could from her so he didn't tramp up that way anymore. I tried to ignore the Minister as the little thing stared up at me, but in time it gave up on getting a response without work and just spoke right up.

A Minister's voice is a strange thing, coming from an animal that you know can't ever speak on its own. There used to be other cats around, when there were more people, and we used to wonder if the Minister could speak cat talk to them, though that didn't seem likely. The Minister was a made thing, not born, and so it didn't meow and croon to the others. They didn't seem to like it at all, I remember from when I was little; nothing could get the cats to move on like the Minister. For humans it was different, since we liked the Minister just fine, and it was nice as nice could be most often, but it made us feel the guilt of all the things we did that we shouldn't have, and there's a lot of that in every life, I guess.

"Your mother is still cold under the table, isn't she?" the Minister said, soft as almost always, a gentle sweet voice like a tiny bird or a girl child small enough to hold in your arms.

I pulled my thread tight and snipped it off, making a neat little knot of it with my neat little fingers. "What do you want us to do? Go out and catch our deaths?"

"The body shouldn't be lying there under the table like that. Not at a time like this."

I looked right at it, into the yellow eyes that stared like nothing else could: not a real cat, not Gospel, and not even one of my old twig dolls that couldn't move or blink at all. I couldn't outstare the Minister, but for a minute, maybe, I could make it see I understood. "Minister, it's cold as death outside, and the snow's near a foot already and still falling steady, and you want my brother and me, as is just now orphans, to go out and dig a grave? You that're supposed to help us, that's what you want?"

The Minister stared right back, though I think it didn't so much stare as just *look*, if I'm being honest. It doesn't manage to blink, or make anything like living responses, most of the time. Made things never could, my mama used to say, but I didn't ever know quite what she had meant. "The snow will only get deeper, Merciful, and the task only harder."

"Do you know how long it's going to snow?"

"A day, and a day, and more than a day more," the silly thing said, which was Ministerspeak for a long time. But the Minister did have a touch for the weather, and knew it well enough: better than me for sure, and better than Gospel, who thought he was clever (and probably was clever enough, truth be told). So if it said it would snow for a long time, I figured that it was right, and I thought of the body in the kitchen and that maybe we should do something after all. Something, but I didn't know what. I really didn't think we could bury it, just the two of us, a not-quite-man and a girl half-grown, in the snow in the dark.

"Can we wait till morning?" I asked. Of course I didn't want to wait. It was wrong not to bury her, and anyway, it gave me the shivers just thinking about there being a dead body about the place, even if it was Mama. "Probably there won't be too much snow under the Big Tree, and we can bury her there."

"Leave her that birthed you to sit and harden till dawn? Ungrateful child, crueler than poison."

And I felt guilty, yes I did. But there really wasn't anything at all I could do on my own, and I knew Gospel wouldn't stir from his bed for anything less than a bear or a catamount or something worse, so it had to be the morning, if I could even convince him then. Morning or not at all, and I couldn't think of *that* because, after all, it was Mama lying there, with her toe sticking out of a hole in her left sock and her long painted fingernails crossed on her chest and her face under our best tea towel.

The Minister waited a silent moment until I turned away from its yellow gaze. I used to be a good girl and do exactly what it said and what it told me, and it liked me better then, I gathered. But since Mama got so sick and I had to be in charge more often than not, I started to feel like it was just bothering me. Only I hated how its eyes staring out at me still could make me feel guilty. More than that, I desperately wished to have someone to tell me what to do—even a preachy little cat what I'd been growing more used to ignoring with every passing year—but it wasn't as easy as all that anymore. The Minister stood up and stretched, for a moment almost what it seemed, and paced purposefully past the chairs and into the darkness of the kitchen. I couldn't hear it, so quiet was its tread, or see it in the dim and flickery light of the lamp, so I just waited with Gospel's pants in my chilled fingers and a needle thrust into the arm of the chair and a spool of Mama's perfect thread on the table beside me, along with a teacup filled with melting snow that Gospel had fetched me when I was working.

It came back and settled down again. "She's growing hard and almost as cold as outside, Merciful. And tomorrow she'll be harder yet, and a load to maneuver. But if it can't be helped, it can't be helped, and dawn is better than dusk, tomorrow better than never." That last was another Minister phrase, one that didn't get much use, but I knew it still. The Minister hopped up to Papa's old chair and breathed two long breaths onto my teacup, and the snow melted and grew to steaming just a little. I drank it down and said thank you kindly both because it was the polite thing for me to do and because I really was grateful to get a little warm into me. The Minister didn't do things like that often.

"You should sleep now, Merciful," the little thing said, and went back over to the kitchen doorway, where it settled down facing into the dark room. Its gray tail swept back and forth, almost like that of a normal cat. I finished the hot water and set down the cup. The pants were just about the best I could do, so I folded them up and put them aside and tucked the needle and thread carefully into Mama's sewing kit. I supposed it was mine now, though that didn't seem right. And still the Minister just sat, staring into the dark, the tail always moving, so that for a moment I thought maybe it was nervous; only that was silly, because a made thing couldn't get nervous.

The light was poor and ruddy in the bedroom, but bright enough to see that Gospel had taken over Mama's bed as someone should have, but it might ought to have been me, since I'd been here all the time taking care of her and he hadn't. But he was older, and anyway, he got to the bed first. Probably he wouldn't stay to use it long, but then, I supposed neither would I, and the bed, the entire house, would go to rot and ruination like so many other places around here.

I tugged out my bunk, the upper one, and then flipped down the supports that my father had built so long ago that I couldn't remember it. The lower bed in the cupboard was bigger, and I was only just still able to sleep in my own. I should probably have moved to Gospel's like he moved to Mama's, but it smelled like my brother, all farts and sweat and greasy hair and wild things, and I hadn't had any time to air it out, so I just hopped on up into my own bed.

"Did you shut the door?" Gospel whispered.

I hadn't, because we almost never did, not since Papa died and the big bed just became a bed, not anything else ever. "No. Why would I?"

"The Minister's out there, not in here, right?"

"Yeah," I said. I wiggled into the quilts and worn sheets that made up my bedding, not caring to climb back down for Gospel's silly idea, whatever it was. Turned out I didn't have to, because he rolled out of bed suddenly and bounded to the door, throwing it shut in a flash. Beyond, I heard the scrabble of claws on the floor, then scratching at the door.

"The Minister wants in," I said softly. In the dim light, I could barely see Gospel, could barely tell he was pacing over to my bedside. His shoulders and head were above the level of my body, and he rested one hand on the frame that held my mattress.

"I know it does. That's why I kept it out. It wants to hear everything we say, Merce. And maybe I don't want it to hear every word I've got to say to you."

"You already said you want to run away while it was there, right in front of us. What's worse?"

He breathed out slowly, completely. "There is worse, Merciful. And I got to tell you, because I can't tell anybody else. And I don't want that made thing to hear, because who knows why it was made?"

"It was made to keep us on the righteous path, the path of goodness, and to tend to us, body and soul." It was what we were taught, and it was what I was supposed to say, and I even think I believed it, most often.

The scratching was almost frantic now, but the door was sturdy wood, and there was no way the Minister was going to get in.

"Come and sit on the bed, away from the door, and we'll talk. I got a lot to tell you. You're clever, Merciful, and I want to hear what you think." He stepped back and flopped onto the big bed, crawling over and away toward the headboard, and then settled down where the light was a tiny bit better, sitting cross-legged, with his hair falling into his face like it always did.

I didn't want to move, finally getting a little warm,

and not wanting to hear whatever cockamamie non-sense Gospel was about to spew out. But he was my brother, and my mother had just died. I had no one else, so I went to listen to him speak, quilts wrapped around my shoulders, on the bed that was almost still warm from the dead woman.

THREE

I DRAGGED THE TAILS OF QUILTS OVER THE WOODEN floor to the head of the bed. Gospel had set himself on the fire side of things so he would be a little warmer, but I had my pile of covers, which meant that would even out. I wished it were switched, though: him all used to spending nights up trees and whatnot, and me a girl who went to milk the goats in the summer mornings and shivered for the chill of it. The Minister scratched something awful as the quilts hissed along the ground, like maybe it thought I was coming to open the door and let it in, or maybe it just realized what we were doing, talking about things it wouldn't like. The Minister heard very well, I knew that much from times when I'd tried to sass it under my breath. I hadn't got anywhere with that, for it would turn its head right quick and tell me what was what.

"We have to be quiet," I said as I sat down on a

pillow, leaning against the headboard that my father had carved before he asked my mother to marry him.

"I know," Gospel breathed. "The Minister's got a lot of problems, but hearing isn't one of them. Whatever they did when they made it, the ears got a lot of it."

"So what do you have to tell me?"

I couldn't see his face at all, could only see the wings of his hair in silhouette from the embers in the hearth, and I couldn't tell what his face was doing, what emotions he was running through in the silence that followed, but I could almost feel that he was suffering through something just then. I didn't reach out to him, because he didn't like me, and didn't like to be touched, and maybe I didn't want to touch him anyway. Not that kind of family, I suppose. It hadn't been for years and years.

"You know how I said that I had gone here and there, seen this and that? Just now, I mean; not all the time, but what I told you out in the sitting room?" It came in slow bits and bobs, tiny gasps of words that forced themselves out past some trouble within him.

"Yeah, I remember. The Hollows, and Windblown Ridge, and up and down the river."

"Uh-huh. I done that, it's true. I went every which way. And I saw just what I said. Only something else, too. . . ." And he fell totally still and silent, and turned to look at the door, so that I could see his profile, the hooked nose and the strong chin, sharp against the light. He sighed out a full breath. "There's an end to things, Merciful. Not like when you die or when a story-book stops. I mean an end."

"What sort of end?" I didn't know what he meant that was different from dying, but he was scaring me a little.

"The first time I went all the far way down the river was two years past, and I went just as far as I said, three days down into the dry country, where the trees don't grow no more. But there used to be farms—you can see the fences still, though it's nothing but weeds. Or, you could see the fences. You can't see anything anymore, now."

"Why not?"

"It's not there anymore, least as far as I can reckon. There's something, maybe, but you can't tell."

"What nonsense are you trying to scare me with, Gospel?" I hissed, and drew up the quilt around me not for the warmth, though I wanted that, too, but because the shivery feeling that I got thinking of Mama lying there dead was only getting worse from my brother's tales.

"It's not nonsense!" he said, only as loud as real talking, but it seemed terrible as thunder after all the whisper and quiet of the night, and there came a single slow scratch from the door that made both me and him stare at it. "It's not," he said, whispering again. There's nothing there anymore, just mist. Mist and cold and a feeling like you've died, and I couldn't dare to walk into it. And last year, in the summer, when I went down the river, I could barely go a day and a half. I walk faster, and my legs are longer, so maybe two days it would've been, the first time. But still, nothing."

"So it was foggy," I said. "Fogs come up sometimes, and then they go away. Did you wait?"

"Did I wait? Yeah, I waited. And the next morning, the fog was over me, and it was cold, and the ground didn't seem like much, like the rocks were worn down and the grass was faded and brittle. There weren't no sun at all, not even through the mist like you'd think you might see, only a glow like moonlight on snow, and I got out of there right away. And this summer . . . this summer, Merciful, not three months gone, I went down the river and there was fog a few hours away, the same damned cold fog." I gasped because he'd sworn. Oh, I knew he did it, and I'd heard it a time or two before, but it was always to make me blush. This was different: just a swear like it was a way to talk. I'd only heard the words used that way by Mama, and only when she was at her worst. "And there was that same feeling like death," Gospel continued, "and that's all that's out there, every direction. I've checked, Merciful, and there's not a damned thing in *any* direction."

"But . . . I don't understand."

"Hell, I don't understand it either. Don't matter if we

do. There's just the fog, and by now I don't know how close or how far away it is. Probably it's right over the hills, so we can't see it, or maybe even closer. With the snow falling would we notice at all, do you think?" He sighed and leaned back against the headboard, his face close to mine. "I think it's the end, Merce. I think it's the end of everything, that fog, and we're really all that's left, for however long until it gets here."

"It can't be everywhere in the world, Gospel. It just can't."

"Yeah, well. They say the world's a big place, so you may be right, but it sure as heck is everywhere around *us*."

"Maybe we can walk through it and get to the other side," I said, though I didn't really much care for the idea.

"I thought you didn't want to leave?"

"I don't. But we got to, right? There's no staying here, if this fog is coming."

He was quiet for a while, and it was warm and almost totally dark and the only real sound was the hissing of snow outside, faint and soft. My mind wandered a minute, half into dreams and memories, mostly about Mama. I think I drifted off then for a bit. Probably Gospel did as well, because both of us shot up full of startlement when the next scratch came, this one long and loud and rattling.

I had put my hand to my mouth to keep from crying out. Gospel fumbled to take my other hand in the darkness that had grown more intense since I'd closed my eyes a moment before.

"That wasn't the Minister, was it?" he asked.

"It sounded like it ran down almost the whole door. I don't think it was the Minister, no."

"Then what was it?"

I didn't say it, but I could only think of one thing, which was Mama's painted nails, and how we should've buried her even if it took all night and got the both of us sick to death. I thought of that, but I didn't say it, because it seemed silly and childish to believe in ghosts, and I didn't want Gospel to laugh at me. "Do you think something got into the house?" was what I did say.

"Like a bear or something? They wouldn't scratch like that, I don't believe. And we'd hear it moving about, I bet. Do you hear anything moving around out there?"

I listened hard for a moment, but I could only hear my own breaths, quiet but sharp as birds' beaks. I was scared, very nearly out of my wits, and I supposed Gospel wasn't much better but had to play it off because he was older and a boy, while I was just a girl and could work myself into a fit for terror if I wanted.

"I don't hear anything," I said after a moment.

"Me neither. So what do you think it was?"

But I still didn't say. I didn't say in case saying made it so. I just held his hand in mine and sat in the dark and hoped whatever it was would go away.

A couple minutes passed, or at least I thought it was a couple minutes. Gospel took his hand away and slid off the bed, quietly but not silent. I guess he wasn't trying to be all that quiet because he tossed a couple of logs onto the embers and stirred them up. I kept my eyes on the door, waiting for something to come through—a deer or a bear or something more horrible—and all I could think was that I'd see her toe first, the one that stuck out of the hole in her sock, but nothing opened the door. The wood flared up almost at once, dry as a bone and ready to burn, and the room got lighter and less scary right away. Gospel took the poker in his hand and walked around to the door, while I just sat still on the bed, useless in my pile of quilts. I was that scared, though. I couldn't move, couldn't barely even speak, though I tried when he touched the handle, tried to call out to him not to open it and let in whatever horror might be on the other side, but all that came out was a little squeak that he didn't pay any mind to.

He pushed open the door. It was dark out there, dark and quiet, and then I screamed when I saw something rush to him and past him, into the room, but it was only the Minister, tail puffed out and eyes wide with what I could have sworn was fear, for just a moment. But then, settled right before me, it looked normal again.

Gospel had swung the poker down at the Minister, though I didn't know if he knew what he was swinging at, and it didn't much matter because he had missed, so fast was the thing at getting up onto the bed.

"Did you do that scratching?" Gospel asked, not even looking at us, still peering out into the room beyond.

"You shouldn't have closed the door," the Minister said, looking up at me as if I was the one who had done it.

"It was Gospel's idea."

"Why did you close the door, Gospel?"

"It's cold, Minister. I'm just trying to keep all the heat in here instead of losing it out into the house."

"You should have let me in."

Gospel turned back finally. "You don't need any heat, Minister. I know that for certain sure. So you were fine out there, doing whatever it was you were doing while I was sleeping earlier."

"It's not right to shut me out, children." And then the thing wouldn't say anything more at all. It closed its eyes and rested its head down on soft gray paws and for all the world looked like a sleeping cat—though, just as it didn't feel the cold, it didn't need to sleep. Not that I'd ever seen. It was listening still, with those clever ears, and it would hear everything we said now. I was starting to think that somehow it had gotten up higher to scratch the door the way we heard, just to get us to open it for curiosity's sake. And we did just what it wanted, I expected.

Gospel looked mad at himself in a way that told me he was thinking about the same thing, but we both knew there was nothing for it. The Minister was right there, and while we could shut the door on it, we neither of us would dare to lay hands on the thing and put it out. Some things just weren't done.

My brother reached out to the handle and started to pull the door closed, this time really to keep in the heat, I suppose. He almost paused when he heard me gasp, a sudden sharp intake, but I gestured for him to hurry and tried to make it look like I was shivering from the cold.

But it wasn't the cold, and the gasp had a reason. Or maybe not. I was almost worked up to a fit, so maybe I was just seeing things. But I almost would've sworn on the Good Book that I saw something, something like a shadow of a person, dim and uncertain, at the far side of the sitting room where the kitchen doorway was, and I remembered that the Minister had seemed afraid. Probably I was just imagining things, but maybe I wasn't. And since there wasn't anything we could do about it at night anyway, and since the door seemed good enough to keep out anything that was scratching at it, I didn't say anything.

But I should have, with all the trouble that later came.

FOUR

THE LIGHT THROUGH THE WINDOW WASN'T SUN, SO I
guessed it had gotten to be daytime but was still storm-
ing outside. Gospel was asleep in the big bed. I climbed
out of my own bed and went to look, pushing back the
curtains of the window and wiping condensation off
the pane. I could see almost nothing but white outside. The snow was still falling at a steady pace, and I
guessed there was close on two feet of it piled up. The
trees across the garden were bent under the masses that
covered them, so that just a few needles stuck out, green
and lonely, and some parts of the trunks, which looked
like muddy stripes on a clean sheet.

It was morning, and I didn't see any better how we
were going to bury Mama. Even under the trees there
was snow; not as much, maybe, but it had been falling
too long and hard for there to be none. And it felt colder,
or at least my fingers pressed to the panes were chilled

through at once, and my breath made the world outside vanish.

I didn't like to think about it, but I was going to have to go into the kitchen. We needed to eat, and that's where everything was—as much of everything as we still had, of course. Some apples and purple potatoes, strings of onions hung up in the cellar, a wheel of strong cheese that we'd been cutting off of for weeks, pumpkins that we brought in when it looked to start snowing. Preserves of various sorts from spring and summer, whatever I had time to get ready between working on the house and caring for Mama. Two squirrels, skinned and ready to cook, that Gospel had caught in snares. And a loaf of bread that I had just finished baking when Mama started her final agonies, and which, in all the trouble just after, we hadn't touched at all. Enough for a bit, but all in the kitchen or the cellar beneath, and I did not under Heaven want to walk in there. Nothing for it, though, since obviously Gospel wasn't going to do the cooking. He barely ate anything but meat nowadays anyway, and that only partly cooked out in the wilds, I gathered.

No choice but to go. I walked to the door and gave it a shove to open. It was bitter cold in the sitting room, so I grabbed up one of the quilts I had slept in and wrapped myself in it, hurrying out and pushing the door shut behind me. The wood floor was icy on my feet, so that I hopped from one rag rug to another, past the chairs, and all the way to the kitchen doorway, where I stopped.

She was lying under the table, just where she was supposed to be, her toe jutting up from her sock, nothing at all moved or out of place. Of course she was. Dead people don't get up and move around, not even if they haven't been buried by their ungrateful children. I tried not to look at her as I kindled a fire in the stove, one that I would be happy to have lit, because it was fiercely chilly in the kitchen. I considered the trip over to the barn to see if there were eggs, or if by a miracle the goats had got their milk back. I thought that maybe we should bring the chickens and goats over here, because it was frigid cold, and they might die. Or maybe already had. But the snow was deep outside, and I thought I'd wait till Gospel was up and make him do it, because it was a thing he'd probably set to with relish, and not something I was looking forward to. Instead, I'd just make something simple for breakfast, potatoes and onions and toast and cheese, and just water to drink because there wasn't any milk. Good enough for a chilly morning like this, when I didn't want to spend much time at the work, and wanted instead to think about what to do with Mama, whom I was drifting around without really seeing.

After the stove was lit, I opened up the hatch that led down into the cellar, flipping it up against the wall next to the door that led out toward the barn, and headed down into the warmer room below. It was a blessing to have a root cellar, cool in summer and warmer in winter, with the earth insulating it, and I loved the rich smell of the onions hanging in wreaths from the ceiling down there. There were bins of potatoes too, and a few withered carrots that I didn't like to eat and never had, and the shelves of preserves that Mama had loved to make, labeled in her neat writing. A few in the front were in my sloppier printing, and probably weren't too good to eat. Somebody had to set them up, and Mama hadn't had it in her this summer. I cut down a few onions and gathered up a few potatoes in the skirt of my dress, then walked back up the wooden stairs with them.

I was so carefully ignoring looking at the body that I didn't notice, until I had unloaded my burden onto the big table—one onion rolling away as always seemed to happen and thudding to the floor, and me dropping to my knees and snatching it up—that Mama wasn't under there anymore. I fell on my bottom and scrabbled back against the wall, almost plunging right on down into the cellar, and could barely breathe for terror. She was just gone, though the tea towel was resting in a rumpled heap on the floor, as if tossed aside.

I wanted to shout for Gospel, for the Minister, for anyone, but the words wouldn't come, and anyways, if she was moving about wouldn't she hear me too? But she must've already heard me: the floor had creaked as I scrambled away, and the stairs before that.

The floor hadn't groaned or protested at all while I was in the cellar. If Mama had moved, or if someone had moved her, I should've heard it. The floors all creaked in this old house. But I hadn't heard anything, and that sure as Heaven made it worse.

I pushed myself up the wall, trying to pretend my legs weren't like jelly from my fear. My breath was coming fast and hard and making fog in front of my face, the room was still so cold. I took a step away from the wall, toward the front of the room, toward the warmth of the fire and the knife block that was on the counter beside it, where Mama's old knives, family treasures and always kept terrible sharp, were settled. If it was Mama moving around, like a ghoul for vengeance, a knife wouldn't do much, but if it was something else, maybe it would help me out.

With my fingers safely closed around the wood handle of a knife, I looked across the kitchen, out the doorway into the sitting room, and lost my grip. Papa's old chair sat with its back to the kitchen, so I couldn't see the face, but a head rested against the back of the chair, hair as dark as Gospel's but streaked with gray, and now, as goose bumps marched up my arms and my skin went clammy, I could hear her.

"Hush, little baby, don't you cry, Mama's gonna sing you a lullaby."

Just the first line and then she was silent. I knew that voice, I knew the song that she sang to me all my life until she couldn't do it anymore, until Mama became a raving thing that sometimes recognized us and sometimes didn't, who most often was harmless and quiet but not always. No, not always. This was my old mama, the soft-voiced one who would sing and read stories and play games, and she was sitting in my papa's chair, which she never used. Not when she was alive.

I wanted to sick up, but I was too scared to make a noise. Except she knew I was there, or why else did she sing at me, why else did she sing that song, of all the songs she knew?

She stirred in the seat as if she was getting ready to turn around, and I ran. I bolted for the back door without even looking behind me or thinking of Gospel, still asleep in the big bed and with only the Minister to look after him and our dead mother stirring not twenty feet from where he was resting, but I didn't care. I just ran as fast as I could, throwing open the door and springing through the snow, through the beastly cold, with a quilt around my shoulders fluttering like a cape and stocking feet turning into ice and the barn looming ahead of me, but I ran right past it.

Widow Cally, that was all my brain was screaming at me. Get to the Widow Cally. I didn't know what she could do, but she could do something, I was certain sure. Or something more than a twelve-year-old girl whose mama was singing to her from past death.

My socks weren't meant for the cold, the chill that already felt like it was the middle of a hard winter, and they were soaked and soggy within a couple of steps. Then my feet were feeling nothing at all. I knew it wasn't good, but I hadn't had the time to fetch boots or even slippers to wear out. No time to do anything but run and try not to scream, though I realized I was praying silently, begging the Dear Lord to save me, to take all of this away and make it like it used to be, even if it meant Mama was still dead. Maybe especially if it meant Mama was still dead.

The Widow Cally lived just a patch away from us, in a tidy little cottage with a cobblestone chimney that was giving up little trails of smoke, so I knew that she was up and the house would be warm. I could tell her what had happened to Mama, and what was happening now, and have a cup of hot cider maybe, or maybe we'd just hurry back to rescue Gospel. I don't know what I was thinking, but that was somehow not the first thing I wanted done. I'd lost the quilt along the way, flying off my shoulders as I ran, so it was just me in my housedress and apron and socks, shivering from the cold, who bounded up on the Widow's porch, where there was barely any snow and her old rocker creaked a little in the cold wind. I pounded on her door, begging her to please, please answer.

The door swung in and there she was, a tall, lean, walnut brown woman with her head inside a knit cap of awfully bright goats' wool and a dress that hung loose on her skinny form. She wore boots inside her house, and costume jewels on her fingers that Gospel and I had delighted in finding for her in abandoned houses when we were younger. Her face was almost as smooth as the one that peered out from her wedding pictures, but now it sagged just a little, and under her cap I knew her long hair was gone but for a few thin wisps that she trimmed with pinking shears. She looked down on me with her brows knit and free hand planted on her hip, and then she reached out and pulled me into the warm of the inside without so much as a word. Esmeralda Cally was her name, but in spite of that she was practical down to her jeweled fingertips, and no way was she going to have a girl shivering on her porch while passing the time of day.

"Child, what in Heaven's name are you doing out on my porch on a frosty morning like this? Is your mother gone badly? Should I come over to help sit up with her?" Because Mama, so far as the Widow Cally knew, was only and always still sick—with her spells and fits and muttered threats, and not dead—if you could call her that.

"Miz Cally, she's not sick any longer, no she's not," I gasped out through chattering teeth while the old lady gathered up an afghan that sat over her padded chair and draped it around me.

"Oh, my dear girl." She said that and nothing more, and then she took me in her skinny old arms and pulled me in tight. I could smell faded flowers on her; I knew she stored her clothes with them in a big chest that came from far away and was carved with animals and roses and vines. It was what a mother should smell like, and all at once I started to weep as I hadn't yet, except for right when Mama died, and then only just a little because Gospel told me not to be a baby. But here I cried and I cried, and I tried to tell what was making me scared and what I thought I had seen, but mostly I just snuffled and sniffled and wailed, and the Widow held me close and swayed a little side to side.

She drew me away from the door after a few minutes of this behavior, and we settled onto a sofa that didn't get much use except for company, not since her son had passed away two years gone. She pushed me back a bit, with some struggle, I'll admit, because I didn't like to let her go. And she took up the corner of the afghan, and she wiped my face, which must have looked a bit of a mess. She waited for me to be a little more calm before she asked what had happened, and why it wasn't Gospel here, who liked the outside more than I did and should've been the one to cross the snowy reach between us.

Somehow I made myself calm down, I don't know how, gulping back sobs and reciting the Lord's Prayer in my head, because for whatever reason that always made me feel better. And after I had run through it once and started on a second try, I felt about able to force out some words.

"Mama passed yesterday, just at sunset. She didn't seem to be any worse, not really, but then she gave a little gasp and started to shake, and her eyes weren't open at all because she'd been napping like she did. And they didn't open again. Gospel helped me hold her down, she was shaking so much, but when it was over, she just let out a breath, and . . ."

"And that was all. Oh, Merciful, I'm so sorry for you and your brother. I wish to God I'd been there, but sometimes these things come on sudden like. But child, what earthly reason could you have for running over in your stocking feet through a yard of snow when the worst is already done?"

And I was afraid to tell her; afraid that she'd think I was a silly girl like I was sure Gospel would. But she just looked down at me from her great height, and she wasn't smiling, because she didn't do that much, especially not at a time like this, but I felt like she was willing to listen, and ready to believe me.

"We couldn't bury Mama, not with the snow."

"No, of course not."

"The Minister said we should, though. Said we needed to put her in the ground to give her rest."

"Minister knows what it's about, I'm sure," the Widow said in a tone that made it clear she was sure of no such thing.

"We couldn't, though. But . . . oh, you'll think I'm telling fibs, but I'm not."

"I've never known you to lie, not since you knew the difference between true and false. You tell Esmeralda what happened, and I'll see if it feels like a lie or not." And she took my cold hand in both of her warm ones, and she nodded at me to continue.

"Mama won't stay dead," I finally blurted out, and tears were running down my face again.

"What do you mean, Merciful? 'Won't stay dead,' what's that mean?"

"We put her under the table, but she's not there now, she's sitting in Papa's chair, and she was singing."

"Oh, child, I'm sure that's just your sorrow making you see things and hear them. I had days when I swore Tom was in the house and that someone had moved his shoes from by the door, but it never happened."

"It did happen, Miz Cally. I saw her."

"Did Gospel see it?"

"He's still abed," I admitted.

"Well, then, we should go and wake him and see where your mama's got to. And I bet the Minister will know more about this than you and I put together, now don't you just think?" And although I didn't want to go back, and tried to tell her that, she shushed me up and got out an old pair of her son's shoes from a great many years ago, and a musty coat, and bundled me up with a scarf and hat, and herself in layers and layers. She banked her fire, and finally we set off, returning through the snow toward my house, my feet still icy in my wet socks.

The back door was banging open and shut with the wind when we reached it. The Widow set her foot to the steps, going before me, which made me feel a little better. She went into the kitchen, while I hovered right on the steps.

"Come on in. There's nothing to be afraid of," she called out, and I stepped up to the door, full of fear, but she was right, it was as it should be. On the table were potatoes and onions, with one onion settled on the floor right up against my mama's shoulder, there where she lay with her hands crossed, a towel over her face, and one toe sticking up through a hole in her sock.

"Is this your onion that you dropped here?" she asked, stooping slowly to pick it up. I nodded. "Well, child, that it rolled up right here against her shoulder, that would be enough to set me to wailing, if it was my mama who was lying there, and bad enough that it's my good friend Rebekkah. But she's still and cold, Merciful, and nothing to be afraid of. Now come in and shut that door. It's chilly outside."

And I did, but I didn't go near to the table, because I had noticed something. It wasn't our best tea towel on Mama's face, though I could see a bit of that beneath her head on the plank floor, where I had seen it earlier. No, it was just a rag towel, one that always sat near the sink, and which, if one had been rushing to get under the table, could've been grabbed at the last moment and laid over one's face.

But I couldn't say something so full of nonsense to the Widow Cally, whose fancy went no further than her jewels, despite what you might think from looking at her. No, I surely couldn't.

FIVE

GOSPEL HAD SLEPT THROUGH THE WHOLE THING, OF
course, and the Minister, curled up right by his head as
if to keep a watch even on dreams, hadn't been disturbed
by anything and seemed not even to have heard the
slamming of the back door, for all the craft of its ears.
When I went into the bedroom to stir them up and get
them ready for company, Gospel shot awake in the bed
at the creak of the door, his hair wilder than ever, the
Minister springing up with its fur raised, making it look
even fatter.

"I went and brought the Widow Cally over to help out
with Mama," I said.

"What's she going to do, help us to dig? We don't need
her old meddling self butting in," Gospel said.

"You hush up, Gospel, and put a polite tongue in that
mouth. The Widow walked over here through a mess of
snow all the way, and I don't want you being rude to her
one bit, no matter who you think you are. Tell him what's

what, Minister, while I see to putting a kettle on and getting some tea for our company." But I felt a little silly as I told him off, because "company" implied something a little grander than just one old lady who was over at least twice a week, anyways. Still and all, he needed to be polite, because this was, really, the only company we ever had, and like as not ever would get now.

Which got me thinking about the mist, and how it could creep right up on us in the snow, and we wouldn't ever notice, and that was a piece scarier than Mama walking around, maybe, and so I shuddered with a little delight of fear and headed back to the kitchen. It was warmer now that the door was shut, and the stove still lit, and Esmeralda Cally had set herself in the wooden chair that we used to shuck peas in when we still grew them, and which Mama had sometimes settled in, even in the last days, muttering to herself and looking at things only her wild eyes could ever see.

"I'll put on the kettle," I said, taking it down from the hook on the wall. Water we had in bucketsful, only there was a skin of ice on it, which told me how cold it had got, and made it hard to fetch out.

"Merciful, you don't need to make any special fuss for me. I know you haven't got but a bit of tea left, no more than I do, and your mama loves it so . . ." She fell silent and looked down at the floor, at what lay there, because she realized what she was saying and that we didn't really need to save up tea any longer after all. In a moment I had the kettle set on the back of the stove, where the fire was hottest and the warm air vented out, and I stood awkwardly, trying not to get too close to the body, because I knew what it was up to when no one was looking.

The Minister came into the room with its tail held high and nodded to the Widow Cally, who gave it a how-do-you-do in return. It paced once around the table, sniffing at the air as it went, pausing by the Widow's chair to give her a yellow stare before finishing the circle just at Gospel's feet. My brother had pulled on his better pants but was still wearing just a ragged shirt that left half his skin on show like some kind of savage, and his hair was a mess, but I supposed the Widow knew our mother was dead and wouldn't think too badly of him, even if it wasn't any sort of grief but his wild side instead. He yawned and nodded his head to the Widow, and that was about all the greeting he gave, so that I wanted to march right over and box his ears. But he wouldn't put up with that, I knew, so I stood by the stove and smiled at the old lady and tried to pretend everything was fine.

"I'm sorry for your loss, Gospel," the Widow said, and she gave a sad little nod of her old black head, and Gospel had the decency to at least look a little affected by it all, and to glance, for just a moment, at the body under the table. "She was a wonderful lady, before she was taken with her spells."

"I kinda remember that, yes, ma'am, I do. Those were good days," he said, and the Minister nodded its feline head approvingly, if a made thing could be said to do so much.

"Now how on Earth are we going to show her some respect, in this weather and all? I don't suppose we could carry her out to your barn and bury her inside, could we? There's no snow there, I'm certain, and the floor's dirt, isn't it?"

The Minister perked up as Esmeralda Cally spoke, and added its own voice to urge that action, which seemed to me like it might work well enough. But Gospel wouldn't have any of it.

"No, ma'am, and no, Minister, as well. She'll lie in the ground next to our papa if we have to wait a week to bury her. The barn—like she was a cow or something. What kind of nonsense is that?"

"Nonsense, young man? It's not nonsense, when this storm might last days, and your mother's poor body just resting here on the kitchen floor like a chicken waiting to be cooked! That'll never do, Gospel, never ever, and you know it. Sure and all it'd be better to have her in the ground next to David, but we can do that later, when the weather turns, and not worry ourselves that she's not got her rest." The Widow seemed less offended than I thought she would've been, but then, it was Gospel's mama who was dead, so maybe he got the benefit of the doubt in an argument right at that time.

I piped up, because I thought it was a fine notion, and I said so. "Allowing that we move her later, Gospel, I think the barn's a good idea for a time. We need to bring in the animals anyway, before it gets too cold for them and they perish of it, so there won't be nothing out there to trouble her." Nor her in here to trouble us, I didn't add, though I saw that the Widow gave me a soft look, as if she knew what was on my mind.

Now it was three to one, and while Gospel relished a fight normally, this was Mama's body he was fighting over, and I don't think he was all that eager to leave it out on the floor, truth be told. With no one to support him, he shook his head and gave way, went to the corner where the kitchen chairs rested till we needed them for supper or somesuch, and took one of them right up to the table and sat down. I noticed he was careful to keep his feet back underneath his seat, away from Mama. There were limits even to his contrariness.

"As long as you're sitting there, Gospel, you might as well set to cutting up them potatoes and onions," the Widow Cally said, and stood to fetch a knife for the task. She passed it on to Gospel, who grumbled but started on the work while I fetched down a pan and we had as merry a little breakfast as one could hope for under the circumstances. The Widow had just a slice of toast and tea, as she had already eaten, but Gospel and I, huddled at one corner of the table, polished off a fair mess of food while the Minister hovered by the back door, eager to be about the sacred work of a burial. It had a prayer for that sort of thing—or rather, a number of them—that it would lead us in, depending on the situation. I wondered, as I ate, if it knew one that fit for when the world was ending and you had to bury your mama in a temporary hole with just one mourner from outside the family and maybe the body doesn't even want to be down yet. I suspected not.

When we had washed up in water that was icy cold, Gospel went to get his winter clothes on while I sat with the Widow. I should've gotten dressed too, I knew that, but I was strangely comfortable in her son's shoes—even with my socks still wet—and the old coat, which was warm enough, though probably not for outside. Maybe I didn't want anyone left alone with Mama's body, just in case. When Gospel came back, in a sweater with a wool coat over it, and his big boots that were actually Papa's and had extra socks stuck in the toes, and with a hat and two scarves because it was truly growing cold outside, well, I realized I needed more than I had and went to go get dressed.

First off I changed out of them soggy socks and into a fat woolly pair that I figured would give me the best chance against all this winter cold. As for the rest, I had more to choose from now than before, because I had set aside the few of Mama's clothes that would work for me, and so I pulled on a lovely blue and green sweater that she had made long ago, maybe before I was born, when you could still get such bright colors for the wool. Over that was her good winter coat, which hung down to my knees whereas it had sat on her waist, but then, she was tall, tall like the Widow, which was part of the reason they had been such good friends, tall women who had felt strange always and with each other at least felt more ordinary. I wrapped a massively long scarf over and around my head and neck before putting a big cap that had been my papa's atop it all and setting out, mittens tucked into a pocket, back to the rest of the house.

Gospel was drinking tea in the kitchen, staring at the Widow Cally as she darned a sock, the very sock that had been on my mother's left foot, which now jutted out naked as a jaybird from under the table. I felt a little shock to see that, almost as much as seeing the different towel over her face (and had Gospel noticed that, I wondered?), but then realized it was only respectful that we not send her to the afterlife with a hole in her sock like a beggar. The Minister seemed right happy with what the Widow was up to, rubbing itself around her legs like a real creature might, and murmuring a satisfied little prayer that I could barely hear, so quiet was its already soft voice.

"Soon as I've got this done, you two can carry her over. I'll get the barn door open somehow, and then we can say a little prayer with the Minister and see her to her rest, for now. It shouldn't take but an hour or so; we don't need to put her too deep in the ground or anything. I do wish we had a coffin, but I suppose there's nothing for it, as it'd take days to get one ready even if it weren't snowing. But, Merciful, you go fetch an old sheet or somesuch, and we'll wrap her up in a shroud. If it was good enough for the Lord, I suppose it'll do just fine for your mama."

Gospel snorted into his teacup, which earned him a harsh look from the Minister but not so much as a glance from Esmeralda Cally, who I suppose had decided to simply forgive everything he did today, in light of circumstances. I nodded and went to the chest in the sitting room, where I dug out the second spare sheets, the fine ones that Mama didn't ever use and I couldn't see us needing.

I carried a sheet back in, and me and Gospel dragged Mama's stiff body out from under the table. It was a clumsy job. I felt like we weren't being very respectful, but then, we were just kids after all and couldn't do it any better. After some grunting and struggling, we rolled poor Mama onto the sheet and folded it around her except for leaving it open where her bare foot was. I shuddered to touch her, but she didn't move at all, gave no sign that she had been singing to me just an hour or two before. I snatched up both towels when we were done, before Gospel could maybe notice, not that he would have cared. He just went back to his tea, which he was drinking an awful lot of. Both towels ended up on the counter, the fine tea towel beneath the rag one, and I realized I was mighty hot in all my layers, in the warm air of the kitchen, and went to stand by the back door, where it was a little cooler.

Only a few minutes passed before the darning was

done, and the sock was slid back over the bare foot and the body wrapped up, all without me so much as moving. Gospel had taken care of the shrouding but then gestured me over, and together we managed to lift the body, him taking the head and me the feet, Mama stiff and unmoving, and the Widow Cally getting the door. The Minister led us out and paced across the snow, somehow not breaking through the surface, though I knew from experience that the little made thing weighed a good fifteen or more pounds. But with such a thing one couldn't say what might happen, and this was just a touch of strangeness on top of the rest. At the barn door, the Widow had to struggle to get it open at all, what with the snow, and in the end we set the wrapped body down on a white powdery bed and shoveled out some snow and eventually got the door open.

It was as cold inside as out, or very nearly, and I knew that would be trouble for the animals. But it shouldn't have been this cold at all, this bone-chilling tooth-chattering knee-knocking cold that even in January we didn't get, and especially not when it was barely fall, even if we were coming off a spell of cold winters. The Widow ducked inside right quick behind the Minister, softly noting how cold it was, her breath steaming from her mouth in a great gout. The goats in their pen were lying down and still, and the chickens were all huddled together with their feathers fluffed out, and after we set Mama down on the hard packed earth I went to check on them while Gospel fetched down shovels from the tool rack on one wall. The goats were cold as ice, dead for sure, and the chickens barely warmer, though the red hen in the middle of the mass stirred when I touched her, so I supposed she was still alive. For the rest, that was all our animals gone, and winter only just beginning, and that was a bad thing. Though if the fog was really coming, and the end of everything with it, I didn't guess it much mattered.

"The goats and all but one chicken are dead, and that one might not live," I said.

"Well, take that one over to the house, and I'll set to digging a little," Gospel said.

"Yes, go on with it, girl, and hurry back to help with the shoveling," the Widow urged. She was pacing about, beating her gloved hands on her opposite sleeves to try to keep herself warm. About that time, Miz Cally must've been wondering, why she was only wearing one hat, a question I for certain was asking myself. It just took me a moment to hurry across the way with the red hen and wrap her up in both the towels and rest her near the stove, where there was some comfort, and then hurry back in time to hear Gospel curse a blue streak.

The ground in the barn was packed down hard, which we expected, but it was also nearly frozen with the cold, which we hadn't expected. But then, we hadn't thought it would get so very chilly in the barn. For all that he jumped onto the shovel with his weight, and pushed and thrust and gave it his best, the ground would barely crack for Gospel. It was obvious after a few minutes that we couldn't bury Mama here, any more than we could outside.

"Told you we shouldn't have even bothered," Gospel said, tossing down the shovel fifteen minutes later, when it was obvious even to the Minister that it wasn't going to work.

"We had to try, Gospel, for your mama's sake. But I guess you're right, it won't happen, and we got to take her back to the house and settle her in there."

And we did, Gospel and I managing the body again, though he was tired and sore and I was chilled right through and the Minister seemed desperate upset, which isn't something a body should be able to tell about such a thing.

"Can we do something with her, instead of setting her under the table again?" I asked as we came through the door.

"I don't know, child. I recall that, once, bodies were laid out actually on the table, and anything less would be awful disrespectful," the Widow said.

"But right here, where we live and eat and all? I don't think I could take that, Miz Cally."

"No, and we shouldn't have to, neither," Gospel said. "Let's set her in the cellar. She'll keep there as well as anyplace, and not be there for tripping over or . . ." My brother didn't say or what, but I think he was as disturbed as I was about having Mama sitting out in the open, though probably not for the same reason.

Strange enough, the Minister didn't say a word against it, though it didn't say anything for it either, but in the end we carried her down the stairs, straining at the job and gasping for breath when we were done. Gospel grabbed up a stack of firewood while we were down there, and we shut up the cellar behind us and each took a seat, chatting for a time before we saw the Widow on her way. By that time the chicken was clucking a little, and I was more content than I had been in a day, and still outside the snow was falling, and the cold was growing, and maybe the fog was closing in, but for a bit, I just didn't care a whit for all that.

Six

GOSPEL HADN'T TAKEN OFF HIS COAT AND HAT OR ANY of that, though he did have another cup of hot tea, and then he announced that he was going out to try to find Jenny Gone.

"What in tarnation are you doing that for? She's hours away without the snow, and you might not make it back here before dark."

He shrugged. "The fog, Merce. The fog might've got to her by now, and if it hasn't, I want to get her out. If it has, I want to know. Either way, it's worth it, unless you just want me to leave her out there." He had leaned in real close to whisper to me, and the Minister was back again on Papa's chair, so maybe it hadn't heard what Gospel said.

Of course I didn't want to leave Jenny out in the wilds dying by her lonesome. I still only half believed him, that there was this cold fog rolling in over the hills and the mountains and the plains and over everything, but it had gone on a bit long for a joke. I didn't think he would try this hard to trick me, not with Mama just dead, even if he maybe hated me. So I told him to be careful and tried to sound like I meant well and surprised myself because I did. He gave me a look that I couldn't quite place. The Minister when we called it said a prayer over him, that he should come back safe in the protective grip of the Lord God and all that sort of thing, and a pretty good prayer it was. A moment later, in a whirl of snow because the wind had picked up something fierce, he was gone.

The instant he was out the door, I took up the heavy chair that the Widow had sat in and dropped it down on the hatch to the cellar. The Minister looked on but didn't say anything, didn't really react except to watch, and I remembered how terrified it had seemed for just that instant when it scrambled into the bedroom last night.

"Have you seen her?" I asked.

It turned yellow eyes up to me but said nothing at all.

"Fine, don't answer. But I think you know something's going on, and that's more than I can say about Gospel, him who thinks he notices a lot out in the woods and can't even see things in his own house. Just don't move that chair, all right?" I said. I thought it couldn't do anything like that anyways, but you never did know.

I pressed down on the chair as if to give it more weight, and then took up the coat I had set off for a spell and went into the sitting room. It wasn't as cold as out-side, that was for certain sure, but it was plenty chilly enough, and I was glad to have the coat. I wanted to be about something useful, and on the loom was a rug Mama'd worked on when she was in a good patch. I'd worked on it the rest of the time, and I thought it would be nice on the floor with the cold like it was, and it was almost finished besides. So I set to the task, not as good as I wished to be, but practice could only improve me, and it at least let me not think for a time about anything but the movement of threads and the clacking of the shuttle. Other than that there was just the sometimes fierce wind outside, and once or twice a pop from the fire in the stove, and nothing else to bother me for who knows how long, since the light never seemed to change and the room stayed cold and Gospel wasn't come back yet.

For a time there was a sound that I didn't even react to, not at first, and then all of the sudden I knew what it was and my hands clenched on the loom's frame and I stopped breathing. For I knew that noise well, knew it and had once loved it, but now it was nothing but dread. It was the sound, soft and creaky, of the rocker in the bed-room rocking away, slowly and regularly, and I had been so used to it as a girl and now, too, that I hadn't barely heard it. Even in her worst days, Mama would take to that chair for a time, and sit a spell rocking, and it made her more calm and biddable for a while so that we could sometimes get her to bed when she was otherwise antsy and fretful. For a minute I thought maybe it was the Minister, what set itself there at times, but then I recalled that the Minister couldn't really make the chair rock, not more than a back and forth when it jumped up, and this rocking was going on, slow and steady, like a body was in the chair. Just like a body was moving it.

And then I heard her singing. *"And if that mocking-bird don't sing, Mama's gonna find you a diamond ring."*

I turned my head and looked over at the kitchen, where I hoped the Minister would be rising up, coming out to find me, protect me, drive away whatever it was, but if the made thing heard anything at all, it truly didn't want to face it and was staying put.

"And if that diamond ring don't shine, Mama's gonna see about a mist so fine."

I moaned for terror, because the voice was just what it should be, but the words, oh, the words. It wasn't just that they were the wrong words, that they were so dreadfully possibly true, but that she sung them just as if she were singing a lullaby still, and I couldn't hardly breathe for a horror that stirred my stomach and made me want to run away.

"And if that mist should cloak the land, Mama's gonna put out a helping hand."

"Shut up!" I screamed suddenly, throwing myself from the loom's stool toward the bedroom door and into the room, and there was the chair, rocking softly back and forth with no one in it, and the fire poked up to a merry glow when I knew it had been low and soft since morning. The bed was turned back just as if it were ready for someone to climb into it. I didn't see any sign that she was there, but still it seemed like the song hung in the air, that I heard her voice singing when it wasn't.

The Minister loped into the room, sniffing with its black, wet nose and stopping, in a moment, at the chair. For just an instant I blinked at it, because it looked so strange right then: big and brown with too-large paws and dangly ears. That was the way it had always looked, but there was something about it, about the Minister, that felt different. It looked back at me with soft eyes and whined a little, and I knew what was wrong. It was as terrified as I was, though I didn't know why it would be, a made thing that didn't feel like a person and was supposed to comfort and protect us, anyway. But I went over and knelt beside it and scratched it along the flank, and it licked me just as you would think it should, if it were really the dog it looked like. For as long as I could remember it had been big and strong and loyal, warm and furry and comforting, and I wanted to stay leaning against it for a long spell, but I needed to be sure, I needed to go and look. And my courage, such a little thing as it was, wouldn't last for long. I needed to go right away, before I curled up with the Minister and didn't move again until Gospel came back to laugh at me, or the fog closed in on us all.

So with my hand on the Minister's head, and it

pacing along beside me radiating strength and warmth, I walked across the cold floor of the sitting room, and into the warmer kitchen, where the hen was pecking around as if there were somehow food on the floor. The big chair was still sitting on top of the cellar door and nothing had been moved out of place, and I felt a mix of happy and confused and scared because it didn't make any sense, and I looked down at the Minister with its tongue hanging a little out.

"Are there ghosts?" I asked it, really softly.

"The dead go to Heaven," the Minister said, which was true but didn't answer the question. Its voice was softer than you would think from such a thing as it was, and not just because it was trying to be quiet, like me.

"But do they ever come back?"

It whined, the Minister who was supposed to protect me and steer me from evil, and I wanted to cry because I felt so lost and alone. I knelt down right then and started to pray to the Good Lord to bring Gospel back lickety-split and to keep me safe and to hold Mama close to Him, so that she couldn't come down and sing to me any longer, couldn't move around, couldn't . . . I don't know what all. And the Minister gave me an Amen at the end, and I realized I had breathed out my prayers loud enough to be heard, but that, I supposed, didn't much matter right then.

I didn't want to be in the kitchen, and I didn't want to sit back at the loom and maybe find myself hearing the song again, so I went into the bedroom, where even if there'd be a bit of awfulness, at least I was far from the worst of it. The Minister paced beside me, tossing a look behind us over its shoulder that made me even more nervous. I climbed onto the big bed and curled up with the covers pulled over me. The Minister flopped down just beside me, next to the hearth, where the fire was still stirred up. I was feeling so fretful and fearful that I thought I'd lie there, eyes open, for hours, but instead, I was dead asleep in minutes.

Seven

THERE WERE VOICES TALKING BUT I COULDN'T MAKE OUT
the words, and for a moment in my slumberous state I
thought it was Mama and Papa, which caused me to jolt
awake all at once and then realize it was just Gospel and
a voice I recognized right quick as Jenny Gone, talking
in the other room. They weren't very loud, and I wondered how I had woken up, but then I thought about what
was in the cellar and I knew. I was scared right through,
and I didn't think I'd ever sleep very deep again, whatever came.

It was barely light outside, the bit of the end of the
day when it got all dim and special, only with snow falling it was just almost dark and nothing pretty about it.
I rubbed at my eyes and then got up out of bed still in my
coat and all. The Minister looked up at me from by the
hearth and then dropped its head back down, but I could
tell it was listening close like always. I paid it no mind
and walked out to say how do you do to the company. It

wasn't quite what I expected, though. Gospel was sitting in Papa's chair, layers piled up around him, looking almost the same as when he had left but for being more pale, like he was a little scared. It was Jenny that was wrong, or different at least, in that part of her wasn't there at all. She didn't have her left arm, and maybe not her shoulder, either; though it was hard to tell because she was all bundled up too. But there was definitely no arm, and there was something wrong with that side of her face, too, which was turned mostly right at the bedroom. They both looked at me as I came in, and I could see what it was that was wrong—she didn't have an ear, though her hair was tucked down over where it should've been. I tried to not stare.

"What happened to your arm?" I blurted out before the sensible part of me could even say a hello.

"And good evening to you, too, Merciful Truth. So glad to be here," Jenny said. Her voice was tart and mean, like she was most times, when she wasn't just out of sorts. She'd got a touch of what Mama had, a bit of wandering eyes and mutters, but not all the time and not so bad when it came on her. It made her right cranky, which was why after the Widow Cally's son died she took herself away. Not that she didn't like people, because she was social as anybody else, but they didn't often like her for long, not even those of us who were used to her. The last time a tinker come through, six years ago, she had cursed him up one side and down the other before he was gone. For a long while we all blamed her for no one else coming, before we realized there maybe just wasn't anyone left to come our way.

"Sorry, Jenny. Hello and how do you do, I see Gospel already set you up with some tea, now what in the name of Heaven happened to your arm?" I plopped down on the bearskin rug as I finished, looking at her with a smile that I hoped didn't show how fretful I was about the matter.

It was Gospel who spoke, and he didn't even answer me. "I found her partway up the mountain. She was already coming down, and guess what? The fog was coming down behind her. Not that I could see it, but that's why she left her place."

"You saw the fog?"

Jenny nodded. "Saw it, went into it, and came out with a little less, if you get my meaning."

I breathed out slowly with terror and awe. Jenny Gone exploring the fog and losing her arm. "How come you're still alive, then?" It was a stupid question, but I couldn't help myself.

"Your sister needs some manners lessons," Jenny said, looking pointedly at Gospel.

"Ain't neither one of us going to give them to her, though. So you might as well answer. You already told me and I'm dying to tell her, only it's your story and you're right here, so I haven't. But if you don't spill soon you'd better believe I will." He seemed pleased with himself, as if he was having a great time now, which maybe he was. Going out into a dreadful storm to save womenfolk was just the sort of thing that would make Gospel's eyes light up, so long as he didn't have to take care of them after. But then, that's what I was for: taking care of everyone. Though not, it appeared, as regards a woman like Jenny Gone, who didn't want any caring for.

"Fine and I will. Now you listen here, Merciful, and don't interrupt, not that it's too long in the telling. It was yesterday morning when I saw a fog rolling in across the hillside, where there's a barren patch with nothing much growing in it, so even with the snow falling and all, I could still see the wall of white moving toward me. Up there, fog'll tend to roll on up the mountain or on down, but not so much side to side, so that was peculiar. Well, I wondered about it, so I got all bundled up in my long coat and a wide brimmed hat and took a pack with some gear in it, because it was that kind of weather. In case I got stranded I didn't want to just be doomed."

Jenny was a good talker, once she got to talking, and I liked to just watch the way her mouth formed the words, each one carefully made and placed by her thin lips: She was probably about thirty years of age, though I didn't know for sure. When I was very small, she still had a pa and was being courted by Benjamin Cally, who was dead these two years now. She wasn't much of a looker, thickset and with hair of no particular color or fineness, but then, there weren't too many choices around neither.

"The fog was cold as a witch's tit," she said, and I like to laughed, only it wasn't in me right then, so I held it back, "and there wasn't no sound that came into or out of it. After just a few yards, I didn't even see any snow falling, though it was thick on the ground still. A deer went right past me, so close I could have reached out and touched it, heading out of the fog. But there was something wrong with it, sure as there's something wrong with me now. It had a patch missing on the flank that faced me."

"A patch of hair?" I asked, and it seemed like it was exactly what she wanted, because instead of cursing at me or somesuch, she smiled.

"No, not of hair. Just a patch, like it was a kid's drawing only someone stopped coloring. Nothing there. Not meat or bones or anything, just blankness. I can't describe it no better than that, and I know that don't make much sense, but it's all I've got to tell about the deer. Now why I didn't just get the heck out of there right then I don't begin to know. I've always been contrary, so I suppose I went contrary to myself. I pushed right on ahead into that there fog even though I knew, I knew right from the top of my head to the tips of my toes that it was wrong and I shouldn't have been there.

"It was only another couple minutes, maybe, till I realized I couldn't see any more tree trunks, even though I was past that clear rocky patch and in among the woods. Or I should've been. No trees, and the ground wasn't seeming exactly white anymore, just . . . well, not white. Like a not-color, but I know that still doesn't make any sense if you ain't seen it. And it was then that I started to get a little troubled, or a lot troubled, because I guess I'd been a little troubled all the while, and I turned and started back. Only that no-color ground was slow to cross and seemed to get thicker, because I must have been pretty far into the fog, and then I . . . well, I can't say I heard something. I suppose it felt like there was some pressure, and I turned to look over my shoulder—"

"Your left shoulder?" I said, perking up on the rug.

"My left. I kind of twisted about as I hurried, pushing my feet forward, and that was when I realized I just didn't have an arm anymore. It didn't hurt. I didn't even feel anything. I guess that's the whole point: I didn't feel a thing, only when I looked forward again there wasn't no arm at all. Nor an ear, but I didn't realize that for a bit longer. I pushed harder than I've pushed ever, and I moved my legs by sheer cussedness and will, and I got out of that fog, only it was right near my house then. I didn't dare go in for anything more, so I just started on down the hill. I come toward here because you're all I know. My pack was flying loose half the time since there was nothing on my left to keep it in, and I realized I couldn't hear so well and that's when I noticed my ear was just gone, vanished." She was crying then, not anyplace but her eyes, just tears coming down, though her voice didn't change and she didn't move at all. Only she leaked out tears the whole time while she was talking, and I didn't blame her a bit. I thought she was real brave, actually.

"And with me only partway down the mountain, there comes Gospel up the hill with a path beat down in the snow from where he'd walked. And we hurry back down, with him not even asking any questions till we get here, and now I've told him, and now I've told you, and I don't want to talk about it no more if that's quite all right." And she took up her teacup with her right hand and had a sip, and then set it down with a clatter, because her hand was shaking that bad. She sniffed deep in the silence that came after her tale, and I felt bad for asking her about it in the first place.

"I told you the fog was real, and I told you it was a terror." Gospel said it soft, and he leaned over to me, but I was sure Jenny Gone could hear it too.

"I know you did. I didn't ever see it, though. How was I to know?"

"Yeah, I guess."

I realized the Minister must have heard every word, because it had come at some point to lie down at the bedroom doorway with its head raised above its paws and big ears cocked up to listen. It panted just like a real dog with its tongue hanging out, and you could let yourself think it was real—only it wasn't, of course. After the trouble we took to make sure the Minister hadn't heard us yesterday, it seemed odd to just let it hear everything, but then, with the fog scarce six miles off I supposed it didn't much matter. The Minister could catch the whole danged story, for all I cared then, because there was nothing left, no time left. In a few days every one of us was going to die, or vanish into something that wasn't, into a cold and dead fog.

Jenny wasn't crying anymore, though there were still streaks on her face. She was ignoring them, and I thought it was good if I ignored them too, like a woman grown who wouldn't pay any mind if her friend's hair was out of place, not till there was a good moment to fix it up. Which this, for the tears, just wasn't. Everyone was looking.

"Does it hurt at all?" I asked finally, because I wanted to know.

"No, it doesn't. There's no pain, there's no blood, and I still feel like I can move it, only I can't. It's just not there. And sometimes I think I hear things from the missing ear, too. Voices, like lots of people talking, but there's nothing there and I don't hear it with my good ear."

"You just can't get enough of this, can you, Merce?" Gospel said with a chuckle.

The Minister spoke up from its post by the bedroom. "That is quite enough of the questions. Miss Gone has suffered enough, I should think." Such compassion in the voice of the made thing. It shamed me to hear it so that I looked down at the rug and picked at the edge of it, where the fur was getting ragged and ratty.

"It's all right, I don't much mind. My own damned fault, really. I should've known it was nothing but badness and left, at least after the deer went by, but I didn't. I got just what I merited, I'd guess."

"No one merits such punishments, nor even knowing of them," the Minister declared, and rose up, walking in its bounding way up to Jenny and laying its great head on her lap like a benediction. Old as it was, sometimes it did the right thing without any call being made, and this was one of those times. The poor crippled woman closed in on the Minister and started to weep freely, like I had with the Widow Cally just that morning. Gospel nodded his head to the kitchen, and I went with him, quietly creeping away to the other room so as not to embarrass Jenny any more than she likely would be already.

In the kitchen, Gospel reached up into the top of the cabinet above the sink, where I couldn't even get my arm to and he had to stand on his tippy toes, and pulled down a brown glass bottle.

"What's that?"

"Whiskey, dope. Papa used to drink it, and the bottle's just sat here all this time. I reckon Jenny could use a swig, and maybe I could too."

"The world's coming to an end and you want to start up with liquor?"

"Ain't like I'll have any more time later. And maybe you should get yours in too, huh?" He pulled out a few little glasses, the sort of thing we never used but had gobs of anyhow, and splashed some brown, smelly stuff into three. He carried one out into the other room, and I watched him set it down beside Jenny, but she didn't seem to notice. The Minister was whispering things to her, I thought, though it was hard to tell over her sobbing. Gospel came back a moment later and took up the other two little glasses, holding one out to me.

"No thank you, Gospel, no thank you at all," I snapped, and pushed the glass away.

"Suit yourself, but I'm betting if Esmeralda Cally herself was here and had heard what we just did, she'd have a plug and call it medicinal." He nodded at me as he set down the glass I'd rejected, and then tipped his head back to gulp down his own whiskey. Which he then promptly spit out in the sink, coughing and gasping. "That stuff is foul. How'd Papa drink it at all, I wonder?"

"Reckon you get a taste for it, probably, same as stewed cabbage," I said, remembering one of my least favorite foods when I was little, though I had kind of gotten to like it before we quit growing many vegetables. That work had become too much trouble for Mama.

"Well, I don't expect I'll get a chance. Shoot. I wanted to be a man who drank." He was disappointed, I could tell, but not as much as he put on.

"Do you think we're really going to die, or go away, or whatever?"

He looked at me eye to eye and licked his lips, and then he nodded real sharp and looked away, corking up the bottle again.

"It's not fair," I said, quiet, and like a little girl.

"Life ain't fair, or Mama wouldn't've gone crazy, and Papa wouldn't've got shot, and you would've had little friends to play with and all that. No, it ain't fair at all." He reached up way high to put the bottle away.

And then I heard it, over the click of the bottle settling into place and the murmuring of the Minister and the softer but still-present sobbing of Jenny Gone. The creak of a step, of one of the steps in the cellar, and my head turned and my eyes flew to where the big chair should've been but wasn't.

"Gospel, did you move the chair?"

"Sure I did," he said. "I needed to get down there with the chickens and the goats, hang them up. I'll cure 'em in a little while, but I wanted to get them in."

Another creak of a stair, almost stealthy, but somehow I could hear it. A few feet off in the next room the Minister had fallen silent, but I couldn't spare a glance to see if it, too, was looking this way. Then I heard the tiniest sound, like a fingernail on wood: *tap tap tap.* Gospel looked over from the cabinet to the back door, where I suppose he thought it came from, but I knew—oh, I knew. It was the hatch to the cellar.

"Put the chair back on top of the hatch, Gospel," I said, trying to stay calm.

"Move it your own danged self if you want it there," he barked, and I didn't even argue. I just hurried past him and picked up the heavy old thing, grunting and straining, and staggered over to the hatch and dropped it there, falling with it just as I swear I saw the blessed thing lifting, the tiniest crack off the floor. Me and the chair slammed it shut, and I plopped onto the seat and shushed Gospel, who was suddenly all interested and full of questions.

I heard the creak of a stair, but it was farther away, and then another, probably right at the bottom, and then nothing. I got on up to my feet from where I'd been sprawled out over the chair and backed away a foot or two.

"Do you mind telling me what the heck is going on?" Gospel demanded, sitting down in the big chair, which right then was about the thing I most wanted him to do.

"You won't believe me."

"Like you didn't believe me about the fog?" His face was a big smirk that I wanted to slap right off of him, but he had a point.

I leaned in right to his ear and whispered real soft, "Mama's up and walking down there."

"She's dead, Merciful."

"I know. All the same, though."

And I stood up, and he looked at me and he laughed a little, and then was quiet for just a moment. He tried to laugh again, but something in my face told him I meant it, meant it for real.

"You're dead serious, ain't you?"

I nodded.

"Well, shoot. I thought the fog was big news, but this is . . . this is just plain crazy. Does the Minister know?"

"I think so. I think it's scared of her."

"I know I am, for sure. If it's really her." He looked down at the door at his feet. "We should go and look."

"No, Gospel, we can't."

"Merciful, there's a fog full of death or worse closing in on us. How bad can it get?"

I admitted then that he had a point and that maybe we should go downstairs, but not aloud. Just to myself. To him and to the part of me that was terrified by the idea, I just said, *we couldn't, we shouldn't, we mustn't*, and tried to leave it at that.

But he was Gospel, and he wasn't likely to listen to any kind of sense, for all my pleading. He just smiled and stood up and started for the sitting room, and I trailed along.

Outside, the light was finally dying, probably for the last time ever.

EIGHT

GOSPEL WENT TO FETCH THE POKER FROM THE HEARTH in the bedroom because he thought Jenny should have a weapon. He still had his knife, though I was hoping we wouldn't really have a need to protect ourselves since it was Mama. Only maybe it wasn't. Gospel came back and pressed the poker into Jenny's one hand, the Minister padding up behind but not really even coming into the kitchen, hardly sticking in its head. I knew—this time I for certain knew—that it was terrified of whatever was down there, even if I was the only other being in this world who could tell there was something to be scared of.

Gospel took aside the chair, setting it back in the corner where it normally rested, and looked to me. I wasn't sure how I'd ended up running things, but I supposed that was because I heard the sounds. Since I'd noticed Mama up and moving, I was the one with experience, same as Gospel'd be in charge and no questions if it were a hunt. So I nodded to him, and he took a moment to start up a lamp, his hands steady like I didn't reckon mine would have been. Then he gripped the hatch and flipped it against the wall. He started down with me following and Jenny bringing up the rear. The Minister didn't even come close, like I thought it wouldn't. It only paced and padded next to the far edge of the table with its head down, whining faintly in the back of its throat. I didn't think to ever see the Minister so obviously afraid, but I guess with the end of the world approaching all things were possible.

The light didn't seem so very bright in the cellar, but it was enough to make out the piles of wood and the barrels for keeping potatoes and apples in and the onions hanging from the rafters, now joined by the chickens head down and two goats strung up by their feet. It was a sight to give me the shudders. Still on the floor was Mama's body wrapped up in the good sheet, only now it seemed like we'd laid her out as a piece of meat just like the animals hanging down above her. The body seemed not to have stirred at all. Gospel went to stand by it, and I came to hover next to him. Jenny kept on the bottom step, not moving into the cellar proper at all, and I didn't blame her a bit. If I'd been through half what she had I'd be upstairs crying and holding onto the Minister and wouldn't let a soul lay any blame on me for it.

"Well . . . it's still right here," Gospel said in barely more than a whisper. "Wrapped up, even. I don't think anything was climbing on the stairs."

"But I heard the steps creak," I said. It sounded stupid and childish even to me when I said it.

"Yeah. It's an old house, and the weather changed so fast I'm not surprised some things are creaking. But it's not Mama, Merciful."

"I knew you wouldn't believe me," I said, and poked him in the side. Inside his words I could tell he meant maybe I was going a little crazy, just like Mama had, and I didn't like that at all. "You're mean and hateful, Gospel Truth, and I don't know why I even put up with you."

"You won't have to for much longer," Jenny said from the steps, and Gospel said pretty much the same at the same time, and that was a sad thing to think on, so we were all quiet for a minute.

"The Minister's scared of coming down here," I said. "You noticed that, right?"

"I noticed it didn't come down. But maybe it just doesn't like to disrespect the dead."

"I tell you it's scared, Gospel. Jenny, did you notice?"

"My girl, you're the one living with the danged thing all the time, and you'd know better than me, I should think." She was breathing really shallow breaths, like she didn't like the smell down here or something. "I'm going back up. You two can figure out what to do with your mama there on your own time." She turned and took one step, but then paused. "Do you hear that?"

I didn't hear anything out of the ordinary, and I looked and saw Gospel was as confused as me.

"Must be the missing ear. Thought I heard a song. *Hush little baby* . . . that one. You know it?"

I gasped and felt faint, leaning into Gospel.

"Our mama used to sing it," he said.

"I don't hear it anymore. Just one moment, I guess. Probably I used to have it sung to me, too, when I was a sprout. I'm hearing all sorts of things I used to hear, now that my ear is gone. Or else I'm going crazy like . . ." And she didn't say it, but we both knew who she meant: our mama, and it was so awkward that she hurried up the stairs.

"I heard Mama sing that song while you were gone," I said to Gospel. I hadn't told him—I'd been afraid of what he'd think.

His mouth ticked up sideways, and I knew he wasn't happy with me. "You did? Did you see her?"

I shook my head, even though maybe I had seen her in Papa's chair, but I didn't know for sure. "She's about, though, all the same. Maybe a ghost, because we ain't got her in the ground."

Gospel shook his head. "There's no ghosts, Merciful. That's only kids' stories. You're probably just missing her something fierce."

"I want to unwrap her."

"Well I don't. So let's just go upstairs and have some supper and figure out what to do about this damned fog."

"You watch your mouth, Gospel, and cut out that cursing. There's no one to care if you're trying to act like a man, let me tell you. And I'm going to unwrap Mama and take a look, whether you believe me or not."

"Fine. Here's the lamp. Come up when you're done." He set down the lamp and almost jumped onto the steps, climbing them two at a time though his legs weren't really quite long enough. I didn't care none that he was gone, anyhow, because he didn't believe me and he wouldn't help me. I didn't know how, but I knew it was important that Mama was singing, that she was moving about, whatever she was doing. Purely terrifying, but important. I knew there would be some kind of sign that she had gone about, if only I could find it. And if I didn't faint dead away, I thought as I leaned in real close to where her feet were wrapped up.

With just the tip of my thumb and pointer I reached for the fold of the cloth there. I was breathing fast and shallow and thinking that the body would move, that she would move even before I touched her, but it didn't happen. I got the edge of the sheet in my hand, and I pulled it down and then flipped it away from her legs.

And there it was, clear as day. There it was. Dirt on the bottom of her socks, both of them: the freshly darned one that I knew was clean or the Widow wouldn't have put it back on, and the other; both of them dirty from the floor of the cellar.

My mama had been walking around.

But it didn't make me feel good to be right. It made me feel terribly alone and afraid because I was down here by myself, and there was a body that maybe didn't want to stay put not a foot away from where I crouched down. The lantern that was throwing light over me and the little puddle of glow from upstairs were the only two things making me not just scream and run off or fall down dead.

The light flickered something wild, as if there was a wind. The sheet was billowing, and the body began moving, and I meant to scream, only a hand clamped down over my mouth, a hand cold and growing too soft, and a voice whispered in my ear, "*Hush, little baby, don't you cry, you know your mama was born to die.*"

NINE

I COULD HEAR GOSPEL AND JENNY TALKING UPSTAIRS, knew they were so close they could rescue me, but it was too late. She had me, maybe had always wanted me from the first time she stirred. I could feel tears on my cheeks, could hear my own faint sobbing, but she just drew the sheet up and around us. I smelled her and only her, the smell of the dead woman going a little bad now, and in the dimness she hummed the lullaby on and on while I wept silently.

Gospel would come down eventually, I knew he would. He would come down and he would see and he'd rescue me. He had to. But he didn't.

The humming continued, and after a while I found that I wasn't as scared anymore, that it was almost like being held in Mama's lap as a little child. Back then it had been me quiet and her humming while she braided my hair or knitted, or later, her just humming and nothing else, because it was something she could still do with her eyes closed to shut out the worst of the world. Now I stopped crying, and though I was still stiff with fear, it wasn't as bad as it had been.

"Are you ready to listen to me, Merciful?" Mama whispered inside the stuffy tent of the sheet. I could tell my own breath was making it that way, because it wasn't her. She was a wrapping of cold all about me, even her hand on my mouth still chilly to touch.

I nodded, and she moved her hand just a little away from my mouth so I could take a deep breath. I coughed from the stench, for sure as sin she smelled a bit.

"I don't know how exactly to begin. I don't know how well you'll understand." It was Mama's voice but not Mama's words, not the way she said things. "Do you know yet that the world is dying?"

"Yes, Mama."

I felt cold air exhaled on my neck, and I guessed the body had sighed. "I'm not actually your mama. I suppose I'm close enough, but not quite. Your mama, she died, just like you thought she did. But I *could* be her, nearly."

"Are you Mama or not?" And I felt like crying again when I said it, since I had only stopped because it was my mama right here, even if she was dead.

"I'm not doing very well, am I?" And that sounded like Mama, if not in the way she said it, then in *what* she said. She used to most times think she was messing things up, even when, as usual, she was doing well. But this Mama, she wasn't making any sense. Upstairs the floorboards creaked a little as Gospel and Jenny moved around, and I was torn between wishing they'd come down and save me and praying they'd leave me be just a little longer. I don't expect it happened very often that a girl got to be with her mama after she'd given up all hope of it.

"Let me try a different way. I'm Rebekkah Truth, just like your mama, only I'm Rebekkah from a different place—like a storybook Rebekkah. I knew your mama, because I could've been her. And when she died, I . . . I found out I could put my mind into her body."

"Are you an angel?" It sounded a little silly to say, but I couldn't for the life of me think of any other way a person could not be the person they were, except to be an angel. The Minister said more than once that angels could come down to us from Heaven and do all sorts of wondrous things, but I never had been too clear on what such a thing was supposed to look like.

She laughed a strange kind of choking laugh and then hugged me tight. "Oh, Merciful, I wish. I really do wish I was an angel. If it helps, think of me that way and think of me as your mother, but I'm not really either. I know a lot about your mother, though. I'm like her twin sister, I guess."

"So you're . . . my auntie?"

"If you like." She hugged me tight for a moment longer, the cool softness of her arms a little unpleasant, but I could pretend it was really my mama for a minute. "You're going to have to be a brave girl, because I need you to do a very important thing. I know why things are going wrong here."

"Do you mean the fog? And the cold and snow?"

"If that's what it seems to be, then yes, the fog. My mind is here, as I said, but this body, it's not mine. Sometimes I'm not even sure I'm in it, and not just dreaming all of this. But I think I'm really here, really holding on to you."

"Of course you are," I said.

Another cool sigh. "Yes. I must be. I don't see everything the way you do, so I can't be very clear, maybe. But I know what's making it happen. And if you can shut off the thing that's making it go bad, it'll stop, and your world will . . . well, I think it'll get better."

"Shut off what? What's making the fog?" Eagerly, I turned my head back a bit so my ear was right by her mouth, wanting her to tell me what to do. Gospel would be so surprised and so jealous, only I realized I couldn't even tell him because he wouldn't believe me. I'd just fix it all myself and smile at him afterward because I took care of everything and he didn't do anything.

"A machine. I don't know what exactly it is, but there's a device that's calling the fog to you, causing it to encircle your home. Whatever it is, the machine is going to run right until that fog devours the world if you can't stop it."

And that was when I got confused all over again. I

knew that word, *machine*, but I didn't really know what it meant. All I knew about machines was that they were for towns and cities, far away and gone now anyhow. "We don't have any machines here, Auntie."

"There is one, somewhere. It might be small, something you just haven't noticed. But your mother knew it was there and knew it was causing all the problems. Can you look around and check?"

At least that was something I *could* do: look around. Maybe there was something out in the barn, something that looked old that I never paid attention to. Or in one of Mama's trunks that I hadn't looked completely through? I didn't even know what a machine might look like, other than a few old pictures in some of Mama's books. "I can try."

"Good girl." The arms that were wrapped around me began to slip loose. "I can't stay any longer. It's hard for me to be here—it makes me so tired. Where I'm from, we don't have much strength. We're dying there, too, but differently."

"You're dying?"

"We all are," she said, so soft I could hardly hear it. Upstairs, I heard a great, huge thump on the kitchen floor like something heavy falling over, and then the creak of floorboards. "Go on upstairs now. There's trouble. Gospel needs you."

And the body slid back to the ground, carrying me in its limp arms still wound in the cold drape of the sheet, so that I was lying on Mama's chest. There wasn't anything left in the body. I could feel that much, and now I knew I was just lying down with a corpse, and I felt like I would be sick. I shrugged the heavy limbs away from me, only they didn't really want to go now. They were all tied up with me in the sheet, and I was whimpering and working at it when Gospel called out my name. I took a deep, foul breath and tried to think—the sheet was really the problem, tying me up, and I twisted to push out from the cloth that seemed to hold me like a net. It was a terrible long moment, but I finally came up for a gasp of air to hear Gospel yelling for me from up in the kitchen.

"Merciful, come quick. Jenny's dying!"

Without even wrapping Mama in her shroud, I heaved to my feet and ran up the stairs, snatching at the lamp as I dashed past. I was in such a rush that I caught the tip of my boot under a step and slammed my shin and my face down onto the wooden slats. The lamp flickered and went out. I lay there for a moment, stunned, then pushed up gasping and climbed the rest on all fours like a dog, as best I could with the blasted light gone out. I winced when my right leg, the one with the smacked shin, set down.

Jenny Gone was on the table, though it looked like Gospel had just put her down there, and he was taking off her coat. I got to my feet and paused, not sure I wanted to see what was under that bundle at her shoulder, but when he slipped the coat loose there was nothing,

nothing at all, just the coat itself that flopped down on the tabletop and her shirt under, except where it wasn't.

"Lord in Heaven," he breathed out. I stepped over, breathing sharp from the hurt to my face and leg, and saw what he saw. When I looked where her shoulder should have been, I couldn't see flesh nor skin nor meat, and I couldn't see what should have been beyond, either. It was just something the eyes couldn't focus on, so it was hard to tell what it was or wasn't.

Jenny's eyes were open, and her breath came fast and shallow, but other than that she didn't seem to be moving or doing anything at all. I took her good hand, but she didn't even squeeze back when I pressed hard. She didn't turn to look at me. Gospel was pushing back her shirt, and I thought to tell him no because it was her chest he was pushing it back over and her breasts that he'd see in a moment, but I was too scared to even talk. He kept pushing and pushing, and from where I stood it just looked like the shirt had been hanging over air, and still was.

"Lord above, Merciful. It's eating her up. I think . . . I think it's right at her heart," he said, and at last there was a hint of pale flesh, and he stopped pushing. The shirt was inches in from her side, and if I had to argue for something, I'd say we were already past the tip of her breast, on the inside slope, maybe. "This's where the heart's at, ain't it?"

I nodded, but he wasn't looking at me and I don't think he noticed anyhow that I had or hadn't answered. I didn't know quite what he was seeing, because he could maybe see where the flesh and the absence met up, and I didn't think that could be a sight for mortal eyes.

"Jenny?" I asked, leaning in real close to her remaining ear.

She didn't say anything, didn't turn her head. I wondered if she had known it was spreading, but then, she said it didn't feel like nothing at all, so maybe she hadn't. Gospel took up the jacket and tucked it back over the part of her that wasn't, and he turned away and stepped to the back door, as if he was trying not to notice a woman was dying a few feet off. The hen pecked around his feet, strutting through the kitchen with soft clucks. I wished I didn't notice any of that; I wished that I just watched Jenny, paid her the attention she deserved, only I can't say that I did.

She called me back quick enough. It didn't take long when the moment came. Her back arched suddenly, her face drew tight, and her hand gripped mine so strongly I forgot about my shin and my cheek that was throbbing, and I hissed in a breath while she coughed and gasped for a moment, and then she sagged, not slowly but like the life had just gone out of her.

And it had. She went limp and she died, right there on the table, with her hand in mine and something that didn't exist eating her up inside. I reached up and closed her eyes.

TEN

I WAS HURTING AND I WAS SORROWFUL AND I WAS suddenly very tired, even though I'd slept the afternoon away like the lazy grasshopper in the storybooks. And Gospel just stood there by the door while I tried to put some order to poor Jenny's twisted limbs—what was left of them—and settle her on the table, straightening out the jacket she was wearing and smoothing down the grimace on her face. I didn't know what more to do for her, poor thing. And all I could think was that we'd all go that way, tomorrow or the next day or soon enough after that in the best case, unless I found the machine and shut it down somehow.

The Minister came into the room at last, tail low, head down. Usually you could count on the Minister when there was a death, but I thought maybe because Mama had been lively it had stayed away, terrified as it was of her. Made me think she was rather unnatural, and she was, I'm sure; but she knew things and was trying to help, which was more than I could truly say for the Minister. But now it came and set its snout up on the table, and then it started to murmur a prayer, and I prayed along with it, and even Gospel could be heard, though he didn't move or look at us or nothing like that.

> *"Heavenly Father,*
> *You made us not for darkness nor for death,*
> *But for life with you for ever.*
> *Without you we have nothing to hope for,*
> *With you we have nothing to fear.*
> *Speak to us now words of eternal life.*
> *Lift us from perdition and suffering*
> *To the light and peace of your presence,*
> *And set the glory of your love before us;*
> *Through the Lord, Amen."*

I didn't know when the words of a prayer had felt more real to me, or when I might ever feel them more than just at that moment. The Minister dropped its head from the table and circled around the body and around me, just as it had with Mama a day ago, and then settled down, alert, by the kitchen doorway, looking at the body.

Gospel was still at the door, looking out through the tiny window mounted in it. It was as dark as the inside of a sack, so I don't know what he was looking at, but maybe he just didn't want to look back at Jenny, and I didn't blame him. I wanted to tell him what Mama had told me, but I didn't think he would listen to me or believe me if he did. And I wanted to search around for the machine, but I didn't even know where to start.

Except I guessed the Minister would, because it was a made thing and came a long time ago from a city. It would know what a machine would be like, and whether there were any around. For sure, with all the poking and prying it did, it would know if it cared to. So I walked the few steps to the thing, and I sat right down next to it, rubbing at my shin as I did, for it still ached. I was sure I had a bruise on my cheek, too, but I ignored that as best I could.

"Minister, do you know if there's any machines around here?"

The Minister stiffened, hackles rising, and stared up at me with wet black eyes. I could hear Gospel turning around off to the side.

"Machines? No, there aren't any machines here. You know that, Merciful."

"Not even a little one someplace?" Even though I didn't think it was going to answer, I asked, because the thing seemed to be losing all control of its reactions these days, and I was pretty sure it was lying to me now.

"There were few machines even in the towns and cities in latter days, and now there must be almost none.

As for these simple farms, you folk never really needed machines, had only a few, and they stopped working long ago."

"So there were machines? Where are they?" Maybe it was something the Minister thought was broke and it wasn't.

"Scrapped, torn apart for bits in years past. There aren't any machines here, Merciful. I've told you."

"Why you want to know about machines all of the sudden, Merce?"

"Just something I heard once, Gospel. Nothing important." I didn't know if there was any point in even looking. Maybe the Minister was right and there was nothing. But Auntie was sure there was, and I didn't rightly trust what the Minister said anymore, so I would have to take a look around all the same.

"You're darn right it's not important. We got us another body here," Gospel said.

"Rest her soul," the Minister added.

"Right, rest her soul, Good Lord watch her. Keep up the work, Minister. But we humans got to do something with it."

"Out to the barn, maybe?" I didn't like to suggest it, but I was kind of feared of what might happen if we just left Jenny where she was. "It'll keep there."

"I don't know," Gospel said. "It's not like we can bury her right now. Down in the basement was good enough for Mama."

"No, Gospel, I don't think it's a good idea, not with Mama," I said, and grabbed at his hand. How hard I stared at him I can't say, wishing and praying he'd understand what I was trying to tell him but didn't want the Minister's floppy ears to pick up.

"Out in the barn, huh?" Gospel said, and his chin dropped just a hint and picked back up after. A nod so faint maybe it wasn't one, but I thanked God quiet-like for letting my brother hear me.

"That is not respectful of the dead," the Minister said.

"Well, shoot, Minister, I don't know that I give a fart for what all's that respectful nowadays," Gospel said, shaking my hand off from his. I was a little shocked, but I was getting tired of the Minister not doing anything and just complaining and fussing all the time too, so I didn't say nothing. Gospel walked over to the table and poked where Jenny's arm should've been. "In case you haven't noticed, things are a little bad right now, and maybe respect ain't exactly high on my list of things to worry about."

"This is the time when it should be highest on your list, Gospel. For these are perhaps the last days. And every human action has weight and merit."

"Sure. Weight and merit. Merciful, you want to help me take this body out to the barn? It's got a lot of weight, and you'd earn some merit with me if you did." And he laughed, a quick bark of a laugh that I thought sounded worse than it would've if he'd cried.

"All right, Gospel." I patted the Minister on the head, which it didn't much like, and I went to grab Jenny's legs. I was getting awfully used to moving bodies, only this one was still limp and floppy, and it weighed a lot more than I would've thought just from guessing. It was horrible, how she dropped off the table, and we kind of had to tug her along with us across the floor and then set her down by the door, me already feeling tired and thinking of how deep the snow was.

Gospel fumbled open the door and we lifted her again, but it was pretty obvious that we weren't going to make any good distance carrying her like we were. "We got to turn around and drag her," my brother said, and I didn't want to but I did just the same because I wanted to get to the barn. So we shut up the house and we twisted her around on the snow, which at least was easy, and then we each grabbed a leg and started to walk with her dragging behind us like a shame we couldn't cover up. I wanted to scream or throw up or at least to curl in a ball and hide, but I couldn't, not then and not later. I had to find the blasted machine and smash it if I could, and the barn was the place to look, I was certain.

The barn door wasn't too hard to force open, what with most of the snow cleared away that morning, and we pulled Jenny in. It was cold—fierce cold outside and almost the same inside—cold like I'd never felt, and I wished I had another coat, another hat, thicker mittens, everything. We pulled poor Jenny into the middle of the barn, in the near darkness, and then stood around, not certain what to do.

"So what was that about machines, Merciful?" Gospel asked, billows of steam almost spelling out his words.

"Mama told me there's a machine that's making the fog come in," I said, not trying to explain all the details.

He blinked a couple times and pushed out his lips. "*Mama* told you that?" he asked.

"I don't expect you to believe me, Gospel. It sounds stupid, I know. But I believe what I heard, and if you've got a better idea for stopping what's happening, I'll gladly listen."

I waited as the mist of my breath cleared away, but he didn't say anything. I was trying to remember if there was a filled lamp out here in the barn, and if there were matches, when I heard one being struck and saw Gospel lighting a hurricane lamp.

"Let's have a look around, then," he said, holding the lamp up above his head.

I wanted to give him a hug, so I did. He reached his free hand around to pat me on the back, which was better than I expected, and then shifted away from me, and we started to look around. The barn was big, had once been meant to hold a passel of animals. Even when I was little there were more: three cows, and some pigs that really lived in the wallow out to the side, and an old, old horse that I loved to pet on the nose when Mama would lift me up that high. So there was a lot more space than we had made use of in the last few years, and bunches of that space was just cluttered with old things. When I was really little and Gospel liked me, we used to play in the barn sometimes, going up into the loft for the short space when we were still friends and my legs had grown long enough, and otherwise clambering in and out of stalls and making forts and suchlike. I thought I'd know most of what was lying about in the place. But now that I was looking with the intent to search instead of just to play, I realized I hadn't seen much of the old junk out here at all.

I remembered the broken chairs piled up in a back stall, though I didn't recall all the detailed carving on most of them, and I didn't recall, even when Gospel told me, that I had broken two of them in a week by jumping up and down on them over and over for hours. The old burlap sacks that had once carried goods shipped up-river from the nearest towns I could remember playing in and with. But the piles of old metal scraps, which I had just recalled as that and nothing more, I now saw were bits and pieces from tools that I recognized: a frame from a loom, hoops from barrels, fragments that looked like they would make a rifle. And other things that I couldn't place.

"Do you think this came from a machine?" I asked, holding up a rusty sheet of metal the size of both my hands put together, with strange bumps scattered on the surface.

"Heck if I know. That ain't familiar to me," Gospel said. "But these gears, these should be from something. Papa told me once we used to have a few plowing machines, that sort of thing, and I bet they used gears. Like in a watch," he said, because at least I'd seen a watch, even if Papa's old one didn't work and was broken across the face besides.

And then we found what was surely a machine, a rusted hulk tucked in one corner, with mildewed cloth draped over it. It had been green, but most of the paint was chipped off, and the metal all rusted and broken. There were gears, and there were things that looked like they would move if they weren't rusted together, and Gospel and me agreed it had to be a machine, though what it might do we couldn't say. It was the only thing in the whole barn, loft and all, that we decided could possibly be what we were looking for.

"We need to smash it up, just in case," I said. I was shaking from the cold, dancing from one foot to the other, and I wanted to get it done and head back inside, where maybe it was a little warmer.

"Waste of time since it's all busted up already," Gospel said.

"Well, there ain't nothing else out here, Gospel, so where do you suggest we find a machine?"

"Over at Widow Cally's," he said, and I lifted a finger to start telling him off but couldn't come up with a single thing to say. He smiled a little and nodded at me 'cause he'd figured out something smarter than I had.

"Do you suppose?" I asked.

"She's old enough to remember machines, Merce. She was around when they still made them, I reckon, so she'll know. And we'll be away from the Minister for a bit, and that can't hurt, right?"

I looked up at my brother, with his eyes half-hidden by the flop of hair that somehow made it out from under all his hats and scarves, and I nodded. "Yes, that sounds about right. And pretty clever, too. When did you get to be smart, Gospel?"

"Can't always be you figuring stuff out. I got a brain same as anyone."

"Don't give much proof of that."

He snorted. "I don't like to show off."

He blew out the lamp and hung it back up, and I started to cover what all we'd searched through, but Gospel just grabbed my hand and pulled me away.

It was a long, cold walk to the Widow's place. Though I'd been over just a while before, it seemed as if it were farther already than it had been. We two followed the fading rut that I had first made in the morning, that Miz Cally and I had made a little deeper coming back, and that I guessed she must have used just the same to get home. With Gospel in front of me, I thought it should have been easy as the alphabet to walk over there by now, but it was a hard slog.

When we reached the Widow Cally's cottage, Gospel stopped a minute at the bottom stair, with his snowy boot set up on it. "What do you mean to tell her?"

"The truth, I reckon."

"Which is?" he said plenty slowly, then bent down to wipe the snow from his boots.

I stared at him, but he wasn't even noticing my glare. "That we need to find a machine, 'cause an angel living in Mama told me that would save the world."

"All right, then," he said with a grin, and straightened up. Gospel shook his head and laughed as he started up the front stairs. "If that's the story. Do you think she'll believe it?"

"She ain't like you, Gospel. She don't doubt a body for no reason except to be on the side of the Devil."

"It's not the Devil making me doubt you, Merce."

"You think it's a made-up story, then? Because it's not. It's the truth, even if it sounds like one of Mama's babbles." How I wished it didn't sound like something she would've said, but oh, it did.

"Well. Miz Cally's heard enough of them kind of stories. She'll squint up her eyes and give you a look and wonder if you're Merciful Truth or not, with a story like that. So you better make it good, because if she don't believe you now, she probably won't ever believe you. You convince her now, or never."

"She'll believe me," I said, but maybe he was right. Maybe the Widow wouldn't think it made any sense at all, and she'd tell us both off and send us away with a paddling. "She won't think I'm fibbing, will she?"

"You're a good girl, Merce," he said, like it was an insult. "She ain't got no reason to think you're a liar."

I frowned, because maybe she did. Not that I had lied, because Lord knows I didn't; only Mama wasn't up and moving when Miz Cally came to the house after I'd come running in a fright, and I hadn't shown anyone the dirty socks that proved she had been. So not lying, no—but maybe she'd just think I was going the way Mama had, into spells and fits and not knowing what was true and what wasn't.

"You gonna knock, or am I?"

"I'll do it," I said, and stepped up into the shelter of the porch. Gospel half a step behind me, I rapped three times on the smooth gray wood and waited, waited and hoped Miz Cally would believe me.

Eleven

The door pulled open and the widow frowned out at us. "What are you doing back here, children? Got the willies from being all alone at home?"

Gospel barked out a little laugh, hard and bitter, and then clapped his hand over his mouth. I shot him such a look as should've curled his hair and shook my head. "No, Miz Cally, it ain't that. Or leastwise not all that."

"Come on in, Merciful. You too, Gospel, but remember you're a guest here, so keep your tongue trained."

"Yes, Miz Cally," he said, stepping in beside me.

The fire was burning huge and bright, and the air was filled with the smell of biscuits, warm and toasty. The Widow glanced into the kitchen as we sniffed. "I thought it would be nice if I baked up some treats and brought them over to help with supper. Truly, I'd have been to your place in an hour at most."

"Shouldn't have wasted the trip, then. It's pretty damned cold outside."

"Gospel Truth, don't think you're big enough that I can't teach you manners."

I didn't really expect him to back down, but Gospel did, bowing his head as he unwrapped one of the scarves that he was bundled in.

"I'm glad you came all the same. The biscuits will be just as nice over here as there, and . . . oh, I don't know, but your house can't be comfortable to you right now." She started for the kitchen, for the big iron stove that was giving off a little steam from the baking.

"Thank you, Miz Cally," I said. "But wait. There's things I got to tell you."

The Widow paused. "More than you already have, Merciful?"

I knew she meant about my mama walking around, and I could hear the doubt in her voice. I looked over at Gospel, but he was busy taking off layers of warmth as if we were going to sit and have treats and talk about how unseasonable it was. "A lot more, maybe."

"Well, let's get the biscuits and some jam, and then you can tell me whatever you need to." And she set to getting things ready, putting out a cast-iron pan full of biscuits on the kitchen table, and a jar of strawberry jam, and knives and little plates and even fancy napkins, while Gospel set aside his warm things and I just stood there with my hat in my hands, wringing it because I was so nervous.

Miz Cally lowered herself into one of the narrow

chairs around the table and gestured us to sit. Gospel dropped onto one and immediately dug into the biscuits, smearing jam all over one and forcing it steaming hot into his mouth. "You'll burn yourself," the Widow said, but without much more than the faintest note of caution. You couldn't warn Gospel off that sort of thing.

"Is it all right if I start telling you what I need to tell you?" I asked.

"Not till you take a biscuit," she said, putting one onto my plate. She stared at me hard until I picked it up and took a little bite. It was perfectly warm and wonderful, but it sat like mud in my mouth until I forced myself to chew up the bite and swallow it. "I suppose that's the best I'll get out of you right now. I don't blame you for feeling so out of sorts, but I do wish you'd try to distract yourself from your sorrows. It's a great help, distraction."

"Miz Cally, there's things a body can't distract herself from," I said.

"I don't know about that. When my husband passed, God rest his soul, I did everything I could to try to lose track of it."

"It's not that, Miz Cally. It's not Mama being gone."

"Well, then what is it? It's not you thinking she's up and about again, is it? I thought that was all settled." The Widow gave me a stern look, the sort that should have sent me cringing into silence, only I wasn't about to shut up now after I'd come all this way.

"I got to ask you a question," I said.

"For Pete's sake, Merce, you're taking forever," Gospel said around a mouthful of the last biscuit. "Either spit it out or I do."

"All right, all right." I drew in a deep breath and let it out slow. "I need to know if you've got any machines around the place."

"Machines? Why do you suppose you'd find any of them around here? They been gone a good long while, Merciful. And what kind?"

"I don't know what kind. What kinds are there?"

A soft laugh came from the tall black lady. "There were all kinds, I suppose. Kinds that did things for us, and that made things; kinds that told the time or showed pictures. I don't even remember all the kinds of machines there used to be, Merciful. They all went away years ago, or fell apart. We didn't need them anymore after the Last War. Why do you want one now?"

"Why didn't you need them after the war?" Gospel asked. It was all stories to him, and to me, those terrible days when folks fought and killed and died for reasons that never much made sense to us. But Gospel, he liked guns and fighting, and he was always keen to ask a question if it might have anything to do with the war at all.

"They never did anything good for us, that's why. We only needed God and each other. We saw what all those machines led to: foolish wickedness, wars, and killing. Now come on, tell it. What do you want with a machine?"

"I can't tell you that," I said, and Gospel sighed loudly, thumping his hand on the table. "Well, I can't. You probably wouldn't believe me if I did."

"Maybe I would and maybe I wouldn't, but until you tell me we won't know."

"Can you just say if you've got any around here? I need to find one very desperately, Miz Cally."

She narrowed her eyes to slits and stared at me, her face hard. I don't suppose she liked to dance and jump for a girl who couldn't say what it was for, but I guessed she was going to give me some leeway same as she gave Gospel, 'cause of Mama dying and all, and I was right. Miz Cally nodded her head at last and stood up, walking back to the sitting room.

"Why didn't you just tell her you talked to the angel, or whatever it was?"

"'Cause she wouldn't've believed me. You said so yourself, and you're right. It sounds foolish."

"Ain't all that different from how you normally sound to me," he said, and leaned back in his chair.

I wanted to kick the legs out from under him, but Miz Cally came back just then with a dusty little box in her hand. It was a pretty thing, made of metal and covered with sparkly bits of glass in all kinds of colors. On the front side, where the lid opened, there was a little metal piece sticking out that I couldn't quite place. The Widow set the box down on the table and then took her seat again.

"I don't suppose there's another machine in the whole village that works. But this one still does, or I expect it should, at least."

"It's so pretty. How come I've never seen it?"

"There's plenty here you two've never seen. This thing I kept tucked away because I didn't want it to get broken. It's very special to me, come down to me from my mama, who died a long time ago, and it was her mama's before that from when she was a little girl."

"Well, what in tarnation is it for?" Gospel said. "Ain't machines supposed to do something?"

"They are, and it does." Miz Cally bent her head in its knit cap over and puffed air across the top of the box, scattering dust. Her long fingers lifted up the lid, which was tall and left a lot of space under, and inside there was a little tiny girl in a frilly dress up on one toe, her arm bent, and a tiny crown on her head.

"What is that?"

"That's a ballerina, a little dancer girl. And this is a music box."

A music box. It seemed magical: all the music I had ever heard was hymns and prayers that we sang with the Minister to guide us, and lullabies, only those I didn't really want to ponder about too much just then. "I don't hear any music," I said.

"Course you don't. It's probably broken."

"Gospel, you can head on home if you don't want to be civil. I'm sure the Minister's got a big long bit of talk saved up special just for you." The Widow stared at my brother, and he stared back. I didn't think they'd ever break it up, so I set my hand on Miz Cally's and shook it gently until she turned her eyes my way.

"How does it work?"

"You just turn the key a few times and then let it go."

A key, that was the metal bit in the front! I knew what a key was, of course: we had one for the front door that hung on a nail outside it, and Mama had showed me how to work it years ago. Once or twice a year I'd lock it up and then go around to the kitchen door and let myself in, and be amazed that I couldn't get out again from the front. I couldn't really understand what it was for, but Mama had said it was to keep out strangers. Since there hadn't been any of that sort around for years, I guessed I'd never need it.

I reached out slowly for the key, but Gospel's grubby hand was there first, turning it fiercely.

"That's not fair. I asked about it."

"You're too blasted slow, Merce," Gospel said, and laughed. Miz Cally slapped his hand away, and the key started to slowly turn back, but I grabbed it and gave it a few more cranks. A single sound had escaped, not too loud, just a little *plink*. I didn't really think it was music at all.

"You can let it go now, Merciful. It'll play."

I dropped my hand to the table and watched. The machine made a faint humming sound, a whirring, and then the ballerina started to spin on her toe at the same time that the box started to make music, real music. My mouth dropped open as I heard it play, and I started to draw in my arms. Why under Heaven was it *that* song?

"What's the matter?" Miz Cally asked, reaching out to take my hand before I could pull it fully back.

"Probably reminds her of Mama," Gospel said. "She always used to sing this song to us. How did it go? 'Hush, little baby' or something like that? Lord above, I hated that song, but Merce always wanted to have it sung to her."

"Oh, I'm sorry, dear," the Widow said, and dropped the lid with her free hand. The music fell silent instantly. "It was a long time ago, but I remember your mama used to come and sit with me, back before either of you was born, and play this box for a while. There used to be all kinds of music—phonographs and radios and that sort of thing—but this is the last I have left now."

The box may have been shut, but in my head I could still hear it plinking along, only there was also an echo like Mama's voice running through my head.

Hush, little baby, don't you cry . . .

I let out a breath that I hadn't realized I was holding in. "Miz Cally, there's something else I got to tell you," I said, and looked up at her. I didn't suppose this was the machine I was expected to find. But it was a sign from God, clear as day, that I needed to talk. I needed to tell what I knew.

"There's troubled times coming," I said, and Gospel, he let out a little laugh but waved his hand for me to go on when I glared at him. "The world's in a bad way, and no mistake."

"Merciful, people have been saying that since I was younger than you are," Miz Cally said.

"Yeah, well, eventually somebody had to get it right," Gospel said. "You gonna tell her quick, or should I just get into it?"

"Get into what?"

"There's a fog closing in on us that's like to kill us all, and it ain't but a couple hours from here at most, and the dead won't stay dead, Miz Cally, and the Minister's lying to everyone."

It wasn't exactly how I would have said it, but mostly Gospel had it right. I was mad he told it out plain like that, so I gave him a look, but it didn't have much venom in it because I guess he said what needed to be said. Miz Cally was looking at him too, but it was a different look: the same one she gave when we used to say we didn't know how the stair got broke, or what happened to the cider.

"He's not fibbing, Miz Cally," I said. "He ain't even told you all of it."

"Well, why don't you two tell me the rest, then?"

I skipped my eyes over Gospel, but he just grabbed the jar of jam and dug his dirty finger into it, and slurped strawberry preserves. He'd got to shock someone with starting it, and now he'd get to avoid the work of actually telling it. So I took a deep breath. I started to talk about the angel in Mama, and about Jenny dying, and about the closing of the world. Miz Cally just clasped her hands on the table, the jewels catching the light off of her lamps, and listened to me carefully, and didn't nod or frown or give much of any sign. Only her brow tightened up a little, and eventually her lips did the same, and then finally I was all done.

"Get your layers on, Gospel," she said. He was running his fingers around the inside of the empty jam jar and looked up at her, startled. "We're going back to your place. I need to speak with the Minister."

She stood up, so tall and narrow and strong, and went to get her things, and I grabbed my one scarf that I had pulled off. Across the table from me, Gospel set down the jar, and then he reached out and put both hands on the music box.

"This's the song Mama sings to you now, ain't it?" he whispered.

"Yes. Yes, that's the song."

He nodded and pulled the music box back to himself, and tucked it into the big pocket in his baggy coat. He put his finger up to his lips to tell me to keep quiet, and I did, but I didn't feel good about it.

Only I thought that maybe we'd want to smash that machine at some point, and maybe I wanted to have it nearby, just in case.

TWELVE

WHEN WE GOT BACK TO THE HOUSE, MIZ CALLY DIDN'T get directly to whatever it was she meant to do. First thing, right off the bat, she tutted and fussed about how the place had got so cold and uncomfortable, and so we built up the fire in the stove and set up candles in the sitting room. The Widow had us tuck rags under the cracks of the doors because that would keep out a little of the cold air. She had brought her last bit of tea, and a bag of odds and ends of food, and she put that all away in our cabinets just like she meant to move in. I gathered, since I'd told her everything, that she didn't mean to go back to her house at all, and I felt a little sad to think that was the last I'd see of the place, most likely. Except that in the back of my head was a notion that the old lady had a way to fix all of this, because why else would she have even come on over?

The Minister just watched from the sitting room floor, big head resting on its crossed paws, all through our odd jobs. It stood up and tromped into other spots out of the way when we needed to set up more candles or get to the front door, but otherwise just stared, and mostly at Miz Cally.

"I don't know that I've ever seen it this cold around these parts," the Widow said as she set the kettle onto the stove to heat up water for tea.

"Don't know that any of us will again," Gospel said. "This is once in a lifetime, for sure and certain."

"It has been getting colder for the last few winters," she mused, pulling down chipped teacups and saucers from the cabinets. I wasn't quite sure what she was about, but Gospel seemed to have a handle on it.

"Yes, it has, at that," my brother said, and I could tell he was holding back a smile. He wasn't the sort to pass the time of day this way. The Minister for sure would notice that much. "But I think this winter'll be the last of the real cold ones."

"Minister, what do you think?" Miz Cally asked, because she knew as well as we did that the Minister had a touch for the weather.

"It will not be much colder than this," the thing said, sitting up.

"I don't suppose it could be, could it?" the Widow said.

"It could, but it will not," the Minister said in its gentle voice, and I could tell that it probably knew better than we did what was happening. The Minister knew the end was coming. It would have been hard not to know, when we were talking about it all the time. And it had such a feel for the weather, surely it could sense the fog creeping toward us. How much did the Minister really know, though? I wondered, did God ever tell it anything, when it was talking to the Lord above about us and our little sins and problems?

"How can you tell about the weather, Minister?" I asked. I realized it had never before occurred to me to ask.

"Some things are just given to me to know, Merciful. The Lord God has shown much of the world to the Ministers, so that we could care for you."

"Didn't do such a good job with Jenny," Gospel said.

"She was halfway to the Devil just as you are, Gospel Truth; halfway, and far enough that she would not have heard words of salvation even if I had spoken them. The Lord's mercy is boundless, but some can't be brought to accept it. No matter, though: I would have saved her if I could."

"Oh, would you?" Gospel said. He pushed back from his chair and stomped over to the Minister, which only looked up at my brother. "*If you could.* Is there anyone you can save, Minister? Anyone at all?"

"Gospel, you sit down," Miz Cally said. There wasn't any fire in her voice, but that made it all the more serious. He turned around with a hard face meant to scare her, but after all he wasn't quite a man yet, and she'd been walking this world longer than both of us combined and maybe the Minister added in. Gospel swallowed and backed away from the Minister and sat back down in a loose sprawl, his hand settling on the worn leather of his knife's hilt.

"What do you know about what's happening, Minister?" Miz Cally asked.

"Even in this world, even in this little village, there is so much happening that I can't begin to answer you," the Minister said. "Do you wish me to tell you about the swallow huddled under its wing in a hollow of the Great Tree? Or about the mole that's dying under the garden? Or that there are still a few pale flowers under the snow, trapped and frozen and perfect but dead just the same?"

"Is that stuff really happening?" I asked.

"That, and so much more. The Lord notices everything, Merciful, and it is part of my task to see some part of it."

"Oh, come now. You're not answering me at all." But if the Widow meant to say more, she didn't because of what happened right then. At first I thought Gospel must have got himself up to a trick to get back at Miz Cally. That was what it sounded like. The little tinny tinkle of notes that made up the music box's song haunted the air all around us. Only Gospel's hand shot into his pocket fast as lightning, so that I knew he didn't have nothing to do with it.

"Hush, little baby, don't you cry," the Widow sang

softly, fixing her eyes on the dog's shape of the made thing. The Minister's head darted from side to side, as if it were looking for a rabbit out in a field. I thought about Auntie lying there still and silent in the cellar and wondered if she was making this happen somehow. Was she dreaming just now and hearing the song in her sleep? "What do you know about that song, Minister? Where's it coming from?"

"Rebekkah was very fond of it," the Minister said.

"It's true, she was," Miz Cally said. "But you don't know where it's coming from now? Or are you saying her ghost is here, making some noise? Is that what you're telling us, Minister?"

It said nothing, ducking its head.

My heart was pounding in my chest, and like the Minister I kept looking around to try to find the cause of the song. But I knew where it was coming from. "We need to break the music box," I said.

"It's not here," Miz Cally said.

Gospel pulled it out and slammed it down on the table. He smirked at the old lady, so that I wanted to give him a clout. I didn't because the Minister suddenly lifted its head back up and stared at the music box like it would at a sinner. Even though the box was closed up, I could tell now that the music was coming from inside, not down in the cellar like I had guessed. I didn't think it was supposed to work when it was closed, 'cause the Widow had shut it to make it stop before, but here it was making those same notes when it was snapped tight.

"You little thief," the tall woman said, and smacked my brother on the side of his head. "That's mine, and it's precious, and don't any of you think of smashing it up."

"But it's got to be the machine!" I said. "It's making the music, the song that I keep hearing!"

"No it ain't, it's just an old music box." Her long arm snaked out and covered the shining shape with a hand big for a woman, and she drew it in close to her on the table.

"But, Miz Cally, it's playing the same song that my mama sang to me! How's it playing that, when it's shut down?" Because we could still hear it in the air, that song.

"I don't know that, Merciful," she said. "I know your mama used to listen to this box playing the music, and she loved it. Maybe it's a sign from beyond the grave, though I don't hold with that sort of thing. The dead are in Heaven; they don't trouble us here on Earth." Carefully, like she was handling a badger or a snake or something that Gospel would've loved, she flipped the lid open. The tiny ballerina twirled about, and the music plinked on.

"Take out the key!" I said. The Widow did, pulling it from the little keyhole, but it didn't matter. The music kept coming.

"Dear Lord who loves us, stop this deviltry," Miz

Cally said, but the music didn't listen. She clapped down the lid and covered the box with her hands.

"If it's so full of the Devil, maybe you shouldn't be touching it?" Gospel said, smirking again. "And if it ain't your music box causing all these tribulations or what have you, then what machine is it?" he asked. "Unless she's got spells coming on her, Merciful got told there was a machine by that old ghost angel." The Minister whimpered a little when it heard that, so quiet that maybe nobody but me noticed. "Though it'd be nice if someone could tell me what the Hell a machine really is."

"A machine's a thing built by people to do things for them," Miz Cally said, and that made me think of something. The brown-furred doggy face of the Minister, only a couple feet away, turned to glare right at me, and I got a kind of sick feeling; suddenly, I was dizzy and had to blink a few times to clear my head. I didn't know what I had been about a moment before, but I caught up with what Miz Cally was saying. "There ain't no other machines around here, child, leastwise not any that work. I got a few broken things over at my house, things we used to have when my husband, rest his soul, was still with us. Not a one that's worked these twenty years or more, and I think most of them are gone to rust and ruin by this time. Maybe you got something here, but I guess you'd know, wouldn't you?"

And then her face scrunched up, as if she was thinking hard. "Minister," she said, and her mouth hung open like she meant to say something more. Then she made a little noise in the back of her throat and set both her hands palms down on the table, and then she fell right out of her chair. Just at that instant the music plinked to an end, and there was a moment of such complete quiet that I could hear the snow falling on the rooftop.

Gospel was up before I could do much of anything at all, up and at the Widow's side and with a hand taking her wrist to see if her heart was still beating. I didn't move, though, because I'd noticed something.

The Minister was staring right at Esmeralda Cally, with its fur all hackled up, and it had been staring at her when she fell, and its eyes followed her down and kept right on staring. I could almost feel something in the air, and I knew the Minister had made her fall. I knew it. So while Gospel felt around at the Widow's wrist, and her feet started to drum on the ground because she had started to shake, I jumped up and grabbed a saucer with a teacup still on it and I threw it right at the Minister, though I cringed to think on what I was doing. This was the Minister, and me throwing something at it like I was a girl still in diapers what didn't know any better. I was grateful that the Widow couldn't see, even though I thought she'd understand in the present moment.

The saucer sailed through the air, losing the teacup, which spilled as it went, and smacked right into the

Minister's neck. Or it should have—somehow it bounced off without seeming to really hit the thing, though the black eyes blinked and Miz Cally's feet stopped their dancing. I was already following right after the dish, heading for the Minister to yank it out of the room like it was nothing more than the dog it seemed, but I slipped on spilled tea and tumbled forward. "Do not touch me, Merciful!" the Minister said, quick as could be, but I was already falling right toward it. There was a smell in the air like after a storm, and as I fell I could feel my hair stand on end, and I landed on the Minister and everything went pins and needles and then dark, and I wondered as it all went away if this was what it had felt like for Jenny Gone.

THIRTEEN

I WASN'T DEAD, THOUGH, OR LEASTWISE I WOKE UP AND it seemed only a moment later. Footsteps thumped past my head, and the Minister's claws scratched on the wood of the sitting room as it scrabbled away. I still felt all pins and needles, though, like I had lain on myself entire and gone sleepy, but it was everyplace at once. My hands felt both numb and hot at the same time. I was for sure and certain falling down a lot today.

I pushed myself up and blinked my eyes over and over, because I couldn't really focus. There was some sort of fierce noise going on in the sitting room, thumping and growling and cussing and I don't know what all, but I had trouble seeing what was happening. Some shape I half-saw was moving around, fighting maybe, and another thing as well, and maybe one of the things was Gospel. I was scarcely able to stand, leaning on the door frame, and I rubbed at my eyes with my left hand. When I blinked them clear, I could see Gospel trying to hold on to the Minister, which was snapping and snarling and being in general a ferocious thing.

"Gospel, keep ahold of it. I'll help you," I said, only I didn't think much about how I would do that. When I moved from my post, I dropped right away to my knees and one hand, hardly keeping myself up at all.

"This thing's got a lot of fight, but I don't think it'll hurt me none," Gospel said. "Not for purpose, at least." He was gasping out the words as he struggled with the Minister. Why it didn't just do to him what it had done to me I wasn't sure, but I guessed what it'd done to me was mostly an accident because of how it warned me at the last. I crawled around the edge of Papa's big chair and saw them still wrestling on the bearskin rug, Gospel's arms wrapped around the Minister's belly, the made thing looking like it was trying to scratch and scrape itself away but couldn't get a grip on anything for all its trying.

I pulled myself mostly up onto Papa's chair, holding to the back and with one knee on the seat and one foot on the floor. My body wasn't so tingly now and I felt almost normal, though my hands were still real hot and itchy. I watched and waited for a moment when I could help Gospel out, for though the Minister couldn't get free, it didn't seem like Gospel was wearing it down or getting any better hold on it. "Don't you do it, Merciful," he called out, but his grip looked like it was slipping and like the thing was going to get loose, and so I moved.

I pushed off of that chair and into the melee, and I crashed into the Minister's snout with an elbow and then my head, which I cracked down on its skull, but I regretted this, as the Minister's got a very hard head indeed. But from there I kept falling, and ended up landing on Gospel's nose, which I suppose must have caused him to lose his grip and let the Minister slip away. Or maybe it just got loose like I thought it was going to, but I knew which way Gospel was going to take it.

And then the Minister did something plain impossible, something I never had seen before. Somehow, without touching it or making any sign, it made the front door swing open. I hadn't thought the made thing could do anything of that sort, had never seen the like, but there it was, the front door creaking wide and bleak wind sweeping the snow in. The Minister bounded for the door while Gospel shoved me aside and lunged for it, only he didn't have near the reach and it was gone into the cold and the dark, gone as quick as lightning. I landed on my side and rolled away into Mama's chair, and coughed and came up to see Gospel's face red with rage.

"Now why'd you go and do that when I told you just a minute before to not do a danged thing, Merce?" he yelled at me.

"I was trying to help! The Minister was getting loose. I could see it."

"It was not getting loose. You just messed the

whole thing up. I could've had it if you hadn't gotten in the way."

"What, wear it down? It's a Minister, for Pete's sake, and they don't sleep and don't eat and don't need rest— how do you think you're going to make it tired?" We were both yelling now at the tops of our lungs with the cold air rushing in, and then Gospel turned and flung the door shut and plopped down with his back against it, glaring at me.

"It don't matter now—the Minister's gone for sure. Whatever you thought it knew, whatever answer it was going to give, it's gone now."

"I didn't have any choice, Gospel. It was making Miz Cally sick."

"How do you know that, Merciful? How in the name of anything holy do you even think you know what the Minister could do? Huh? How?"

He was so angry, his face like a beet and his eyes wide and wild, and I remembered that he didn't much like me and maybe I shouldn't have given him another reason not to, but I had to do it. There was no answer to his question. I just knew the Minister had been up to something bad, but I didn't know how I knew. Which is what I told him.

"Just knew, huh? Well, that's swell. Why the Hell don't you *just know* where the danged machine we're looking for is, then?"

Again I got that kind of dizzy, sick feeling in my head

when he said that. Something about knowing where the machine was that we were looking for, only it made me feel wretched just thinking on it, so I didn't. "I think Miz Cally was about to tell us, and that's why the Minister used its power to shut her up."

"And then didn't use it to stop me wrestling with it?"

"Look, I don't know everything! Maybe whatever Miz Cally was going to say was really trouble for it, and you wrestling it wasn't any danger at all? It got away quick enough."

"Thanks to you," he said.

"I didn't mean it to go that way, Gospel, and you know it! But doesn't matter how that turned out. What I mean to say is that the Minister was doing something to Miz Cally. I bet she's fine now that the Minister's not here anymore."

Gospel snarled and pushed off the door to his feet, holding out a hand that gripped mine with harsh painfulness. I was yanked up so hard that I almost lost the feeling in my arm again, and he dragged me out to the kitchen. The Widow was laid out on the floor, but it was clear right off she was breathing.

"See, she's not dead or nothing," I said.

"No, but she ain't awake neither."

And I couldn't doubt that; nor could we get her to wake up, for all our trying. I thought maybe we should move her to the big bed, but she was tall and we were tired and, anyway, Gospel said he wasn't about to shift such a weight. So instead I just fetched a cushion from Papa's chair and set it under her head, and draped a quilt over her. She seemed fine to both of us except for not waking up, but then, we weren't neither of us so skilled in physic that we knew all that much.

The house was colder even than it had been before, and I could see snow not even melted on the sitting room floor where it had swirled in. It was a little warmer in the kitchen, but the Widow on the floor not two feet from where Mama had been laid out made us a little less than comfy, so we both without a sign made our way to the bedroom. Gospel set himself on the bed and I climbed up into Mama's rocker, and we sat quiet and ignoring each other for a time.

"Way I see it, we got two choices right now," Gospel said eventually. "And they're both stupid ones. Either you can go and try to talk to Mama again, not that I'm saying there's anything to talk to, but maybe there is. Strange things are going on. A ghost angel might not be the strangest." I was pretty surprised he came even that far in not making fun of me or just acting contrary, so I held back any smart words that I might've let loose. "Or else I can go after the Minister. It's mighty cold out there, but I don't reckon it'll go all that far—it ain't likely to just vanish into the forest or anything. Only reason it ever got very far away was to look after some trouble for people, and there's no folk left but us here, maybe in all the world. So probably I can find it, I guess."

He didn't seem all that eager, though, and I didn't blame him. The wind that blew in had shuddered my skin from just a hint of touch, and me still in a coat and boots and all. I didn't even want to consider the outdoors, and what it would be like in the dark and wind and snow out there. I didn't much like the other idea, though. Whatever was in Mama wasn't much help, either because I was too simple to understand it or it was too different or something; and anyway, I was starting to think that Auntie was maybe lying, or maybe wrong, because it kept talking about machines and suchlike when there weren't any to be found. But I guessed there must be some truth under the mistakes or lies or whatever they were, and if I talked to Auntie, maybe I could get to the bottom of it.

I really didn't want to talk to her. There wasn't a way to think about it that made it a good idea: either she was a dead person talking to me, and that wasn't in keeping with the Good Book; or else I was touched in the head and going the way Mama did, which was a fearful thing to ponder. I didn't feel like I was losing my mind, but I suspected that wasn't a thing you really noticed.

Sometimes we all had to do things we didn't want to. "I'll go down and see if she's back. Probably she is since we heard that music. She got real tired and couldn't talk to me anymore before, so maybe she won't be able to. But I'll try."

"You do that." Gospel hadn't looked at me while

he was talking at all, just watched one of the candles'
dancing flames instead.

"I'll be going now," I said, slipping out of the chair,
which creaked back and forth behind me. Gospel didn't
turn, and I decided I didn't care. I walked calm out of
the room and then ran with my boots thumping and the
floor creaking across the sitting room and the kitchen,
right to the cellar door. I crouched, taking a moment to
look over at tall Esmeralda Cally lying there and make
sure she was still breathing, which she was, slow and
steady. I stood back up and grunted and strained to move
the big old chair off the hatch.

"Hey, Merce?"

"What, Gospel?" I expected he wanted to complain
about how much noise I was making or something just
as stupid.

A long silence. "You be careful down there, now.
Come on back up safe."

I drew in a long, raggedy breath, half a gasp and half
a sob. I glanced over my shoulder at the kitchen doorway,
but I couldn't see him: he was still on the bed, I supposed. "I'll do my best." And then I lifted up the hatch
and propped it open, took a deep breath, and called down,
"Mama? Auntie?"

I thought maybe she'd move if she was there, but I
didn't hear nothing at all, so I guessed I'd have to climb
down. The lamp we'd gone down with before was still
there at the top of the stairs, and I lit it with a punk from

the fire in the stove, pardoning myself to Miz Cally for standing right over her while I did so. She didn't seem to mind any, so I headed for the stairs again, careful not to trip as I went down slow.

I was getting to be an expert on degrees of cold, and it felt especially chilly down in the cellar 'cause we'd had fires going upstairs long enough to feel almost warm. Still, the cellar's cold wasn't a patch on that blast of winter that poured in when the Minister leapt out, so I kept on downward. Mama was still there, unwrapped and with the sheet pooled around her, just as I'd left her. One arm was flopped out to the side where I had pushed it when I was getting loose, and her mouth and eyes were open. I couldn't move any closer when I saw that. I felt like I had so often in the last day, like I wanted to be sick, and the smell, which was stronger than the earth and onions of the cellar, didn't make it better. I almost went back up and told Gospel I couldn't talk to her and he'd have to go out, and wouldn't that serve him right? I couldn't, though. Hate me or not, he was my brother, and I'd never send him out alone into the cold night unless it was needful and certain. So I stepped down all the way and over to the body, and I knelt down by Mama's head, careful not to touch that floppy arm, and I tried breathing real shallow while I leaned over her.

"Auntie, are you there? Can you hear me any? I found a machine, but I don't think it was the one. And now the Minister's gone wild, and I think it knows what machine we're looking for. Can you hear me? Can you help?" My breath misted out to moisten her face. I knelt there, looking at my hands, which were red from whatever the Minister did to me, I supposed, and thinking about how I didn't want to die and just wondering what was going to happen.

"I guess you can't hear me. But if you can and just can't say anything, we really need your help. If you can make it back here and tell me anything more, I'll do whatever you want me to. Even Gospel, I think he believes in you too. So we'll do what we need to, if you just tell us what it is."

Still nothing at all. The cold outside was waiting for Gospel, and I didn't want to tell him I hadn't tried everything, so I put my hand on Mama's shoulder, which was getting kind of soft, and I shook her. I didn't think it would wake her or anything, but maybe Auntie would notice it better than my voice. It seemed stupid, that I was shaking my dead mama's shoulder to get an angel to talk to me out of her mouth, and for a moment I wondered if I wasn't, in fact, just plain crazy. But I didn't have anything else to try. Nothing happened, and I pulled my hand back and wiped it on my thigh.

"Fine. Don't do anything. And when Gospel goes out and dies in the cold, it's your fault for not helping me."

I reeled back as breath hissed out of her lips. The air didn't mist at all.

"Are you here?"

"Only for a moment." Like a whisper forced through a door, that's how quiet it was. I leaned in close to hear. "So tired. Find the machine. It's moving. Always moving."

"It moves?"

"It's a machine, Merciful. They have moving parts—some of them move. This is one of those," she said with an edge to her voice I hadn't yet heard from Auntie. Mama had carried that edge around a lot. I started to get mad, because how was I supposed to know that machines moved? Machines I'd seen were just pictures, and pictures never moved none. But I thought of the little ballerina, and it moved when the box got wound up.

"Is it the music box? The one that plays the lullaby?"

"What music box? No. Oh, God, it hurts," she said, but I didn't think she was talking to me. I wanted to do something to help her, but there wasn't anything I could think to do. It like to killed me how much she sounded like my real mama did in the worst of her spells. A shudder went through the body there on the ground, and Auntie gave a little cough and then started to speak again. "I don't know what it is, exactly. Your mama saw it, but she saw it as all different sorts of things, and I only saw hints of it through her. She was a little crazy. You know that." The voice was getting quiet, like she was moving away from me.

I knew it. I didn't need this thing to tell me. "Well, what do you think it looks like?"

"A cat," the voice said, fainter, "a dog." Which made me think of something. I remembered the front door opening, the snow billowing in—something there, a shape, but it was like there was a pressure in my head and I couldn't focus on it. I closed my eyes, dizzy for a long second, and then blinked them open. What had she been saying? About the machine? "Maybe a bird. Or a squirrel? Have you ever seen one of those?"

"Yes, ma'am. We have them in the woods, leastwise when it's not snowing up a storm."

"Look for that," she said, so faint that I had to lean in close to catch even a hint of the words. I felt no wind coming from the lips, only a faint, sickly sweet smell that made me pull back now that she was quiet.

I didn't know what she wanted me to look for any more than I had before. There were clues: it moved around, and it looked like an animal, and my mama had seen it. Something tickled at the edge of my mind, something I knew I should know, but it wouldn't come to me for all the trying in the world. Something . . . something the Minister had said, maybe? I got really dizzy again for a minute and couldn't remember what I had been thinking on. I blinked and frowned, feeling frustrated. I couldn't figure it out.

But I knew where a bird was. One that moved around, and one that Mama had seen. That old hen that had lived through the cold, and didn't that just make it seem like it was unnatural? I surely knew that it felt like a real living thing, and that it had laid eggs and clucked and scratched, but I couldn't for the life of me guess what else it could be.

I wished Auntie'd said something useful about the Minister, and why it was playing its tricks, but it didn't matter now. We didn't need to worry about the stupid old thing. Let it play outside in the cold; we'd stay warm inside and make Miz Cally better and stop that moving machine. It'd be easy now that I knew what to do. I just needed to find the hen.

Fourteen

I CLIMBED THE STAIRS WITH PURPOSE, HURRYING UP
them like when I was a little slip of a girl. Killing a hen
was an easy thing, something even I'd done a time or
two, though I didn't relish it like Gospel did. I couldn't
recollect the chicken getting out of the house when the
door was open, and didn't think a machine would have
been stupid enough to go out in the cold, so she had to
be around somewhere. But any old normal hen could
and would get into strange spots in a new place, and it
might take a while to find the creature even with Gospel
helping.

He was sitting on the floor by the Widow when I came
up the stairs, staring right at where I appeared. "Did you
talk to her?" he asked me when I stepped up into the
kitchen.

"I did. She wasn't too helpful, but I figured it out." It
felt like a brag, and maybe it was. If he thought I was
messing up, I really wanted to make sure and rub it in

that I knew what was going on. "It's an animal, Gospel, one that Mama saw. It's got to be the hen. That hen lived through the cold, and that's not a normal thing."

"That's plain silly. Thing was near dead when we brought it over here, and no mistake. And it's just a clucker, nothing special. I think you heard wrong, Merciful."

I was right tired of him not believing me, no matter how obviously right I was. I thought I should just tell him that, but there wasn't much point, I was sure, because he didn't care. So I started to poke into corners and make scratches and clucks like another chicken, to call the creature out.

"You're not seriously looking for it that way, are you?"

"The Lord knows I am. And you sure as your hope of Heaven should help me." I didn't look up at him or anything while I set to searching, and probably that made him mad, me ignoring him.

I heard the smash of metal on the floor and turned to see Gospel stomping the heck out of the music box with his boots. Bits and pieces of the thing scattered all over the floor, coming to rest against the cabinets, on top of the hatch to the cellar, right up against the Widow lying there quiet and peaceful.

"There. That's your God-damned machine, all right? So it's done, and we're done, and we don't have to worry no more."

For just a moment I thought maybe he was right. It seemed so silent and still right after, with all the little pieces shining in the light, the jewels that were only glass sparkling, the ballerina without her legs lying right in front of me.

And then the music started up again, the tinny tinkling coming from the floor, from every bit of the cracked-up box. Plinking notes rang out, not quite as clear as they had, but it was still the same song. I fell back against the counter as the ballerina started to turn on the floor without a sign of how it was moving, as if it were still in the box, still attached to the machine.

"Make it stop, Gospel!"

"I'm tryin'," he said, and brought down his boots again, those heavy boots that my father had worn right up until he got himself shot. But nothing Gospel did made a difference: the music just kept playing on and on, though the little fragments got littler and the jewels got smashed up into dust and the bits of the ballerina couldn't even make themselves turn over any more.

I dropped to my knees and clasped my hands. "Oh, Lord, forgive us sinners, and save us from perdition, and please, please make it stop."

"He ain't listenin', Merce!" Gospel said. He plunged to his knees beside me and shook my shoulders. "God's not paying any attention to anything down here. Can't you tell that?"

"Lord, forgive my brother. He's a sinner, but he don't mean to be wicked."

"Hell I don't," he said. "Now stop your praying."

"You better pray with me, Gospel, if you want this to be over," I said. I reached out and grabbed his arms and brought his hands down from my shoulders, and I clasped them in front of him. He could've stopped me, but he didn't. "Now pray with me. Just say the words after I say them."

He frowned and his eyes narrowed. His hair had fallen down over the left one. "Dear Lord, preserve us from evil and from wickedness," I said, and Gospel said it after me. I don't know what all I babbled then, prayers like I had done when I was really little, begging and pleading and trying everything to get God to listen, and Gospel just went on saying whatever I did.

But the music didn't stop. God wasn't listening.

"Well, all right. I guess it's Your will, then. Thank You anyway." Gospel didn't say that part, but he did chime in with me when I finished with an Amen, and right then, right as we said that one word, the music stopped playing.

"See? You see? God did it. He shut it off."

"You think God did that? Why didn't He shut it off when you asked, then, if He was going to do it anyway?"

"Because we weren't done praying yet. I don't claim to know what God's about, and why He didn't stop it directly when I asked. But we said 'Amen' and it stopped.

Why else did it happen?" Sometimes I wondered how deep Gospel was in his wickedness.

"Aw, Hell, Merciful. I can't believe you're so gullible." He pushed himself up from the floor. "Do you think it ended?"

"What?"

"The storm. The fog. All that stuff? 'Cause we broke the machine?"

"That's not the machine," I said. I pushed myself up and walked the few steps to the back door, and I pulled it open, just a crack, to let the the furling edge of the blizzard whistle in, and then shut it right fast. "No, sir, that wasn't the machine."

"Fine." He kicked at the little bits and pieces, making up a pile of them by the water bucket. "Let's find your damned hen, then." His lips pursed up, and he looked mad as the Minister did back when we used to pull on its ears, but Gospel helped me look. He searched around the kitchen in the cabinets and such, because even if you think a chicken couldn't get in them, you would probably be wrong. But the blasted thing wasn't in the kitchen. It wasn't in the sitting room either, when we went to looking there for a long spell that involved turning over everything in the room, looking in the baskets of sewing supplies and the chests and under the chairs where their fringes swept the floor. And then I knew of course that it had to be in the bedroom, only I couldn't find it for all the looking I put in.

After a time, Gospel pronounced himself completely stumped and bothered, since it was just a silly old hen, and how could it get away from us, anyway?

Of course, there was one place we hadn't looked, and that was in the cellar, where I had started the whole thing. I didn't figure it was too likely that it could have happened, a hen sneaking past me, but the thing wasn't anywhere else, so eventually, in the midst of all the disorder, I said I'd head back down and have a peek. Gospel got a look of such relief on his face that I realized he had figured out a while ago that it wasn't just a hen, but something clever enough to creep on downstairs, and was too blasted scared to tromp on into the cellar. I wanted to shame him for that, him being the older and a boy besides, but then I decided it was a bit silly to trouble him when he already knew. I suspected it was shame enough to see me go down there again, my head high and unbothered.

Even after just such a short time, the air below seemed colder then I expected, though perhaps that was just because we had been moving so much abovestairs. In spite of the brave thoughts I'd had about showing up Gospel by being bold, I was still getting the shudders all along my spine. The body was lying there quiet and still, but who knew for how long or whether, finally hearing me, Auntie might sit up just when I started searching around?

I couldn't help but stare at her for a bit, with the

shroud half around her. For a minute I imagined that the fingers of one hand were closing, but I blinked and couldn't see them moving anymore. Lord, how much of a fraidy cat was I, seeing things in the dark like I was still seven or eight? I mumbled prayers to myself as I started to go around and around the room, holding up the lamp to see into corners.

After I'd felt all around behind the barrels and crates and had started on the piles of wood, I realized there was a spot among all the logs that I couldn't get to with my hands because it was too far back in the corner. I just knew the hen was hiding back there in that little dark nook, waiting for me to go away before it came out with some strange machine satisfaction at having tricked me, and no sir was I going to fall for that. I set down the lamp and clambered up onto the logs, scratching my shin. It hurt because right there was where I'd bruised it before; I bit my lip to keep from making a sound that maybe Gospel would get a laugh from, thinking I was scared down here.

I stretched back to the hidey hole, and there she was: the little chicken for sure hiding from me. I could tell then that she must be the machine because of her hiding in the cold like that. It made sense, the machine making the cold and hiding in it and living while all the rest of the animals died in the freezing barn. I wondered why it had taken me so long to figure it out. And why else would the stupid thing have taken itself to such a strange place, a little cubby among big logs that I was having trouble reaching into, except because it knew we'd be looking for it?

The wind picked up fiercely outside, hard enough that even in the cellar I could hear it. *Hhhhhhhhhuuuuuuuuu*, it sounded like, just like a long breath let out, like the world was exhaling.

Eventually, I got a grip on the creature and pulled it out. I didn't have a hatchet or anything to kill it with, so I was going to have to take it up to Gospel and have him do it. But then, maybe I could just stomp on it and break it up, like the music box? It felt like a real animal, but the angel in Mama said it wasn't and so maybe it would break. I guessed it was probably better to just treat it like it was a chicken, since it had spent years laying eggs and pretending to be a bird. Gospel could kill it, like he'd done to the stupid cluckers so often before. Only fair, really—since I'd done the finding—that he should do the killing. I crawled back, cradling the hen in my arms, but then it started to peck at me and struggle, which it hadn't at all when it was getting caught.

"Stupid hen, just come on and let me get you out of here," I said to it, pulling it in close, and then with a burst of energy it slipped out from my grip and fluttered away toward the stairs and bolted up them lickety split.

"Gospel, she's coming up toward you!" I shouted. Then I realized what else he could think from that and added, "The hen, I mean."

I dropped one foot to the earth and felt something under it. Right away I stopped, because there shouldn't have been anything there at all, unless a log had tipped, and I'd have heard that if it happened. Slowly I turned my head and looked down the length of my body. And there she was: Mama, lying on the ground with her arm outstretched like before . . . but it was stretched a lot closer to me, and her eyes were open and looking at me while her lips moved without noise. The tip of my toe was right on her hand, and I flinched it up and away.

"Merciful," she said, or I think so, because her lips moved that way. I couldn't hear if there was an actual word because of the darned hen clucking and Gospel yelling up a storm.

"Are you back?" I asked, still holding my leg above her hand, which was shifting slowly toward me, the entire body twitching as it moved closer.

"Back?" she said, this time with a little noise that I could hear because the hen chase had gone on into the sitting room, sounded like. Nothing more was said, though, and it was starting to be scary again. This didn't seem quite like the angel who had talked to me before, the one who was but wasn't Mama. *She* could actually speak, and whatever was in Mama's body now didn't seem to have the knack.

I leaned back until my bottom was on the woodpile and crabbed away on the stacks, which were falling away under me. The logs weren't placed in a good way to hold up a body, but I had to try to get away without going inside her reach, and sideways over the woodpile seemed the only way to me. Slivers sunk into my hands, but while I sucked in breath, I didn't stop moving until an entire section fell away and sent me tumbling down with it. And then her hand, dragging her body with it like an anchor, clamped tight on my foot, and I did scream for real, a horrible loud scream like I had just been beaten. She had a weak little grip, but it was a horror that a body was holding on to me, not a person. Leastwise, I didn't think there was a right sort of person in there.

The hand, for all the loose grip it felt like it had, still pulled me closer, because there was just logs under me that rolled right along, carrying my body with them. The other hand came up to take my other leg, and my wailing became nonstop then as I tried to grab at anything to slow myself down, only again it was just logs all around, none even too big or heavy because they were meant for the fire. So I grabbed one and tried to twist around and beat on the closer of the hands, the one what had just got a hold. I didn't have any too good a position and couldn't get much of a better one, so I didn't hit harder than an infant might, and she kept right on dragging me.

I heard footsteps on the kitchen floor, and then Gospel was coming down the stairs with a bloody hatchet in his hands. "Merciful?"

"Gospel, help! She's got me!" And I was a little

ashamed at how gratified I was to see him leaping down the last steps and springing over the fallen wood and lifting up the hatchet over his head.

"Gospel Truth, you put that hatchet down this instant," the body said, in a tone that was weak as a kitten but still purely echoed Mama when she was in a mood, in the days before *everything* was a mood. And my brother did just what he would have done then, he paused and he looked shamefaced and he didn't do what he'd been told to; but he didn't not do it, neither. The hatchet just hung there, red and steaming. Gospel's hair was a shadowy cowl around his face, his breath panting. At least I'd stopped screaming, though she still held both my ankles.

"You know who I am. I know Merciful's told you. I'm here now, completely here, in this place for good."

He looked at Mama's body and then just past it to me. "Sweet God Almighty, she does talk," he said.

And here I thought for sure he'd believed me. "Yeah, she talks. She moves around. She does all kinds of things, just like I told you she did."

"I'm sorry. I thought I believed you, but . . . there's believing, and then there's seeing. Should I get you loose?"

"I expect she can let go of my legs any time she wants. And now would be a good time."

And she did just that, so she could use her hands to push herself up like she was rising from her grave. It was awful to watch, because her skin was all discolored where she'd been lying, and this was really the very first time I'd seen her moving around much. It was horrible. All the joints seemed to be a little loose, with the skin bulged out, and there were purple markings on half her body that looked like bad bruises. Her eyes were milky, and her lips were dry and tight, so that her mouth didn't quite shape things just right.

"So is it you in there, Auntie?" I asked, because she sounded and moved so differently from before.

"Oh yes. No place else to be. The world I came from, it's almost gone. I must be dead there, same as your mother is here. Which means that this is where I'll stay. Until the end, one way or another."

"I'm sorry I didn't believe you, Merce," Gospel said from the stairs.

I gave him a quick nod, but that was all the time I could spare him. "You're dead?" I asked Auntie. I didn't know angels could die, if she was an angel; and if she wasn't, well, I hadn't really thought if she was living or not. I was almost up to my feet, moving away from her and toward Gospel across the tricky woodpile. He was finally lowering the hatchet.

"It's not that simple: dead and alive don't mean what they used to. But yes, you could say I am. There isn't enough left of *me* to be alive, is maybe a better way to phrase it. I needed to join with what's left of your mama, with this place and what strength remains here, to keep even as little life as I still have."

"So some of Mama's still with you?"

"Oh, I suppose so. She and I were very close in a way. I know a lot of what she knew, so I guess you can say some of her is with me. But really, it's just her body: even dead, it's stronger than mine was alive. Where I was, the world was growing very . . . thin, very frail, and all of us who lived there were doing the same. I don't think most people even noticed, but I could see your place here and I knew we were dying, even if everyone else said I was mad." The sagging face shaped itself like it was trying to grimace, but it couldn't quite do that. I put my fingers in front of my eyes, peeking out through the gaps, because no human being should look like that.

"It doesn't matter now, though. I'm here. We must find the machine and destroy it. Then it'll get better. The worlds will right themselves and it'll all go back to how it was." She had raised herself and drawn up her legs while she spoke, and was trying with wobbling limbs to push to her feet. I felt like I should help, but couldn't bring myself to reach out to her. She was still powerful awful.

"I broke that machine. Or killed it, I guess," Gospel said, holding out the hatchet with the gore of the hen still on it.

She achieved her feet and stood there unsteady, her

milky eyes looking at the hatchet. "That's blood," she said.

"Sure is," Gospel said with a laugh. "You should've seen how much that damned clucker bled. All over the place in the sitting room, though at least I kept it from running around."

"You killed a . . . a chicken?" she said. I started to feel like maybe I had been wrong, though I couldn't figure out where I messed up.

"Merciful said it was the machine."

The dead gaze turned to me, and I couldn't hardly stand it. "Where did you get that idea?"

I swallowed hard and clutched my hands behind my back. It was like we were doing lessons again when I was little. "You said it was a bird, an animal."

"You children. I'm glad I'm here now. Glad I can take matters into my own hands." The filmy eyes drifted toward the red-stained hatchet in Gospel's hand, and maybe Auntie tried to smile but it was hard to tell. "The machine was here in this house. I could tell it was here when I was still in my world, but it's gone, I believe. It's so much easier to know what things are now that I have eyes to see. It was shaped like . . . a dog, perhaps." When she said that, it made me think of something, like a word that I just couldn't remember was on the tip of my tongue. I opened my mouth like I was about to speak, but there weren't any sounds that I could put together. All the time now, I was getting these strange feelings, like when one of your sums won't come out straight. I wished I knew why. But Auntie kept right on talking, not taking any notice of me or my troubles. "And now it's not. Now it's different. I don't know any longer. But it's *changed*." The last word was stretched out and strange to hear, almost like I was listening to something foreign, though I didn't know any foreign speech.

"Changed how?"

"It must have changed even as I was naming it. This machine is something that's been here a long time and knows this world. It's smart, you understand, not just a *thing* with a *function*—you don't just press a button and something happens. It's a complicated device, this machine. It doesn't look like . . . why am I bothering? You don't have a frame of reference for any of this. So: it moves, it can think. And it knows you two very well, I suspect."

"A thing that moves? There's nothing here that moves except me and Merciful and Miz Cally. Oh, and the Minister, I suppose," Gospel said with a laugh. Blood was dripping slowly off the hatchet.

"I'm starting to think the Minister's no use for just about anything, Gospel," I said. "But whatever the machine is, it can't be moving. She's probably wrong. Whatever she wants to say, she just got here."

"Right. Except for how you been listening to her this whole time," Gospel said.

"Well . . . yeah. I didn't have anything else to go with."

"Quiet!" Auntie said, wheezing her breath out in one long, dragging word, then sucking air back in like she was pumping a bellows inside her dead chest. She sounded so much like Mama that we both turned to look at her, and I finally noticed something that had gone by me till now: there wasn't any mist in her breath like when Gospel or me talked. "The Minister. What is it? What does it . . . do?" Auntie asked, her head craning forward and tilting a little right.

"It doesn't do a God-damned thing when you need it to," Gospel said.

"It's supposed to look after us. Only it's not very good at it. It's old, and I think it's a little crazy."

"But what is it?"

I blinked at her and gawked for a minute. I looked over at Gospel, but he seemed just as confused. Finally, I just shrugged. "It's the Minister."

"That's not an answer!" she said, and reached for me. Gospel lifted up the hatchet, and Auntie fell back a few steps.

"You get over here now, Merce," Gospel said, calling me over with his free hand. "I don't think I like this version of Mama any better than the real one."

I sidled over to my brother's side. I didn't want to say anything disrespectful about the one who birthed me, so I didn't, but I was for sure and certain thinking the same thing as my brother. And the way Auntie looked was, allowing for the body being a bit turned for the worse, just about the same as Mama had when she was in one of her spells: her face twisted, her hands bunched up. In the eyes, even milky white as they were, I could see the same thing I'd seen so many times in Mama's.

Madness, pure and simple, and if I didn't like to think about it, it didn't matter. Sometimes God didn't give you no choice.

Fifteen

THEM EYES. I'D SEEN THEM SO MANY TIMES, SO MANY ways. When I was little, they didn't show up at all, or leastwise I don't remember it. But by the time I was six or seven, with Papa killed so it was just the three of us and more often maybe even just two, I would see them all the time. Mama'd be sitting at the loom and then she'd give a little gasp and she'd turn and look at me, and there they were. Or we'd been making up preserves, and then I'd know I had to leave her alone in the kitchen, because she'd turn such a stare at me that I shivered. And it wasn't just the eyes.

Mama spent a lot of years talking to people we couldn't see, and seeing things we couldn't either, and sometimes doing things that didn't make sense. At first it was harmless, or so it seemed: just a few words to herself. She would stop what she was doing and say something, but it wouldn't be at us, that was pretty obvious. Then she'd go right back to knitting or milking or telling a story, whatever it was, and if we asked her what she had been talking about, which we did at first, she didn't know exactly what we meant, but she would get angry all the same. I tried to pretend it wasn't happening, after I realized it was a touch peculiar. I figured that out, even young as I was.

Gospel, being Gospel, had to bother at her and me about it. That just made her angry and made me sad, which—Gospel being Gospel—was probably about what he expected. This went on for some months, until I was crying most nights because Gospel kept taunting me, and Mama was hard-faced whenever she saw him. He went around feeling put upon because nobody liked him and ran off a lot to learn woodcraft from Jenny Gone. He was only ten, but he'd vanish up into the hills for days on end.

The spells got worse, and sometimes Mama would carry on whole conversations, only one side of course, that would last for minutes at a time. You could make some sense of them, at least in the fact that it seemed as if someone could've been talking back. But no one at all was there. Sometimes Mama would start to move in strange ways, like she was climbing stairs or opening doors that didn't exist. And it made her mad, because she didn't recollect anything she had done. But she always noticed *something* had happened, for sure she did. Time had passed, things had changed. The tea water might be ready when it had just been set to boil, or the sun might have vanished behind a cloud, or the fire might be suddenly roaring when it had been dying down a moment before.

She didn't know what was happening and didn't want to listen to Gospel because he never had anything good to say, or me just 'cause she was cussedly stubborn. She would get angry with us both, and then sometimes she would go outside and sit alone for hours, or close herself in the bedroom. We didn't neither of us know what to do. Gospel went away more and more. Which left me and Mama and her spells.

The Minister had never been much help with her. In the beginning it still had rounds to do, visiting local folk and seeing to their problems, and so it missed much of the strangeness at first. But when things got worse and worse, and there were fewer and fewer people to see to, it still didn't do much. Sometimes, to be fair, it would touch her with its tiny paw; her eyes would start back to life and she would know where she was and what was happening. I had no living idea why the made thing didn't do more for her, because if not, then what in tarnation was it made for after all? Why didn't it heal her like that more often, or just medic her all the way better? It was a Minister, made for our aid and comfort, and should've done such a thing. It never did, though, just watched and spoke calmly now and then to me or to Gospel when he was about, telling us "This, too, shall pass" and other fairy-tale stuff that I tried so hard to just accept. I prayed more and acted better so she'd get well again. But inside I felt like for all the trying and believing the Minister was failing us all. Sometimes Mama couldn't even stand the little made thing—she'd throw something at it, or try to get a grip on it and weep when it slipped away from her quick as could be. She'd used some pretty ripe language about the Minister, but nothing worse than what I kept to myself whenever it ignored her problems.

And then of course, because that's the way of things, those problems got ever worse and worse. There was less time when she was Mama and more when she would sit, sometimes talking, but sometimes just still and silent, her eyes jumping around at nothing, her hands shaking or pointing or what have you. I'd lead her to bed then, which was easy enough, as she moved along pretty simple. It got to where you could leave her there for hours and just spoon-feed her and make sure she hadn't messed the bed, which she didn't, often. Only rarely was she Mama again, and then she'd be angry but mostly at herself; Gospel'd get his hair cut and the house would be spic-and-span and socks would be darned. But that was less and less often. Usually she'd walk around or yell at things, or act like she was climbing, or building, or running from horrors that no one but her knew the whereabouts of.

In the last months, it was sometimes all of that stuff at once. She'd be Mama, but she'd be talking sometimes to people who weren't there, and it made her angry and sad and ornery, and we had to deal with it. I had to deal with it, I suppose, since Gospel would just go out hunting or whatever when she got bad. In those last days the Minister couldn't even come in the room without her snapping at it, calling it names like I ain't never heard before, and so it kept out of the bedroom pretty much all the time in those last days. In the end it really had been just Mama and me, no Minister, and certainly no Gospel.

If Gospel hated me, I guess it was fair to say that I mostly hated him, too. He left me alone with her for years, and I hadn't forgotten it, not by a long shot. And I was still the one who had to deal with Mama, even now that she wasn't Mama at all.

"Do you know what made her go mad?" I asked the body.

Those horrible dead eyes closed up slow as sunset, and I thought maybe she was gone, Auntie, but then she started to speak again. "She was aware of me. She saw what I saw, and lived what I lived, some of the time at least. It must have been very different, very strange for her. Maddening," she said, and made a noise that I guessed was supposed to be a laugh, only it was terrible to hear. "I wasn't aware of her, not much. I had strange dreams now and again, dreams where I lived in a cabin in the woods, dreams where I had a husband and children. Such strange dreams."

"That's not what your life was like?"

The head shifted back and forth awkwardly, like it

was hardly connected to a body. "I can't really explain to you what my life was like. I lived in a city with millions of people, and I was a doctor. I worked with machines and science—things you don't even know about here. And your mother was smart enough to know it was different, but not quite smart enough to understand it. I think maybe my life, my existence, might have made her mad." The voice was rasping out now, so harsh and rough that the words weren't terrible clear.

"Gospel, go and fetch some water for our guest. Her throat must be powerful dry by now, with all this talking." I could see that her lips were starting to crack from moving so much, and her tongue looked swollen and rough behind her teeth.

"I ain't leaving you down here with that thing."

"Fine. We'll both climb on up and down all those stairs, then, and me with bruises and scrapes all up and down my legs."

If he noticed I was sassing him, he didn't act like it. "You first, then, and I'll catch you up if you stumble back." His eyes hadn't left the body the whole time, and the hatchet was still in his white-knuckled hand. I thought he probably wanted to hit her. I'd tell him that wasn't the right thing, only I was sure he wasn't likely to listen to me. So instead I just backed up a pace or two to the steps, and started up them with Gospel following behind, him slow creeping up the stairs like he expected that feeble monster there to spring up after us.

Thinking on that, as I filled a jar of water from the bucket, where it was icy cold but not quite frozen, I wondered why she got so slow and clumsy. Before, she must have moved real fast to get back under the table, and so on, and now she could barely move at all. I wondered if the body was just getting worse off, only it hadn't been good anytime, being as it was dead.

"Don't go back down yet. We need to talk," Gospel said, grabbing my arm as I headed for the stairs.

"About what?"

"About that thing. And what it said. We ain't killed the machine, it said."

That part I hadn't wanted to think about. I couldn't think of any other animals it could be—everything was dead, unless there was a fly on the wall or somesuch. "Yeah. I guess we ain't yet."

"Well? What do we do now?"

"We take her the water, and we ask her."

"Hell with that, Merce. I say we find the Minister and make it tell us what it knows. This thing downstairs, it don't know nothing good, I'll tell you that."

"And you think the Minister is better? After what it done to Miz Cally?" I gestured at her, out cold still. "You think it would even help us, after all this?"

"It's a better plan than yours," he said, and set his face so I knew he meant to go after the Minister whatever I said. Since I knew it and he knew I knew it, there wasn't much more to say. I started back to the stairs, and he let me go. I was down only a couple when he stalked off, thumping his boots on the floor extra hard.

"Don't forget to close the door behind you, Gospel. It's really, really cold out there!" I shouted after him. It was mean to say, but he'd made me so mad that I just couldn't help it. And then it was too late to take it back or say I was sorry because he was gone. So I prayed inside that the Lord God would keep him safe and bring him home, and that he wouldn't get eaten like Jenny Gone or gobsmacked like the Widow. With such a small space of world left, I thought the Lord would hear me extra loud even without the Minister to help me out.

It was right there, Mama's body, Auntie. I didn't know quite what to call it—no, *her,* because she was a woman and I was certain of that. There she rested at the bottom of the stairs, with her back on the wall and her legs sprawled out in front of her and her arms the same. Her eyes were open staring ahead, and her mouth partway open too. I put my right foot really careful on the floor between her legs, my left still on the bottom step, and made sure I wasn't touching her at all. With both hands I held the jar of water and leaned it in to her mouth, tipping it slightly. The head turned up a little to take the water, and it flowed into her. She didn't swallow, she didn't gulp, it just flowed like I was pouring it down the drain, and then it was gone.

"Did that help?"

"A bit, yes. But I don't really have the muscular control

to handle such things. I'm new in this body. Before I was just visiting in dreams: I moved like you do in dreams. Do you know what I mean?"

I nodded, because of course I knew dreams. And I guess it sort of explained how she got from place to place like she did. "But how's that work? You might have been dreaming, but I was awake. This isn't a dream, this place here."

"I don't know for sure. If you made me speculate, I'd say that this world is more like a dream than you imagine, Merciful. But now for me, the same as you, it's real. And I can't just run fast as the wind, or float from place to place. Now I'm stuck here, trying to figure out how this body works. It's like moving into a new house: you don't know where anything is, how to turn on the lights. It's taking time is all."

I couldn't figure properly what she meant, because nobody I knew ever moved from their house, but I nodded anyhow. "Well, it's good to be a help to you," I said. "Now I'm going to need you to be a help to me. I need to know what this machine really is." I plopped my bottom down onto the stairs, resting my chin on my hands and elbows on knees.

The white eyes drifted up to me. "I told you it moves and it changes. Is there anything like that here? Because whatever it is, that's the machine."

"Nothing ever changes here, leastwise not till just now."

"I wonder if you're right. I think more things change than you know."

"What's that supposed to mean?" I wished she would just make it more clear, because I surely couldn't get my head around it.

"A dream, remember?" That was all the answer Auntie gave me before she went to something else instead. "As clear as you can, tell me what's the Minister."

"Servant of the Good Lord, doing His work here on Earth," I said promptly, because that's what the Minister was, officially. Not that we called it that much, but that's what it was. "It leads us in prayers and does the services for the dead, consoles us in times of troubles, and keeps us on the path of righteousness." It sounded a bit much when you said it all together like that.

"You keep saying *it*. Where I'm from, ministers are people, men and women."

"Oh, no. It's not a person at all. It's a Minister. I guess there's all kinds, but the one here, it was made to look like a squirrel. I guess because we're out in the woods and all."

The ghastly face leaned forward a little, the hands curling up like fat white spiders. "Was it always a squirrel?" She thumped her hands on the ground and let out a little growl.

I scooted up a step to move away from Auntie. "Yes, of course. It's always been that way, long as I can remember." Just for a moment, then, I felt dizzy, and in my mind

I saw something else: a big brown dog, like the one we used to have. Only we never had a dog, nor a little gray cat with yellow eyes that would sit in Mama's rocking chair . . . but for a minute I knew we had, somehow under the sun we had. I rocked forward, my head aching fiercely like I'd hit it on something, and the dizziness got so much worse that I felt I was going to be sick.

I closed my eyes and said the Lord's Prayer, holding my hands on my temples. Blood rushed around my body. Now I half remembered times I'd been scolded by a dog, or heard Gospel get prayed at by a cat, and it was so strange, because I knew all of that was wrong. I couldn't tell what was a memory and what was a fancy.

I took a deep breath and opened my eyes. Auntie was still there, right in front of me, not moved at all. The world hadn't changed. Except that it had.

"The Minister's the machine," I said.

"Yes," she said, water bubbling out of her mouth to spill over her sagging chin. "I believe it is. But why do you think so?"

I turned my head away from her, grimacing and closing my left eye so I couldn't see her face any more. "I can . . . I can kind of remember now. That it used to be a cat, and a dog, and . . . and I think it was other things, long ago, when I was littler. And it knows about the weather—it keeps saying how the cold is going to get only a little worse and then it'll be over. Only how in the Good Lord's name does it do what it's doing?"

"Because it's got real power, some kind of . . . magical power. It prevents you from knowing, from understanding. *Magic*—how stupid I feel using that word, but I don't know what else to say. And how obvious, now that I know: a made thing, a machine, what's the difference? Nothing, to me. But to you, there's a world of difference in those two items. Maybe because of the same power that keeps you from knowing it changes form." A sort of sigh came from Auntie, and it wasn't as bubbly sounding as her voice had been. I peeked open my left eye and saw that there wasn't any more water running from her mouth.

"Do you know when the Minister came here?" she asked. The lumpy, swollen hands had started to move, forming into fists and then releasing. I couldn't help but stare at them. "I'm just practicing, Merciful. Getting to know my new home. Answer the question, please."

"Fifty years ago, just about. Mama wasn't even born yet, but she came along soon enough after. The Minister did the baptism and everything." I almost laughed, wondering how a squirrel could have done that, or even a dog or a cat, but there wasn't enough bravery in me to laugh when the body was right in front of me, looking powerful wrong.

"And why did it come here?"

"'Cause of the Last War. God was angry and we needed guidance, so the Ministers were sent to guide us into a better path. Everybody said it worked—we ain't had no wars since then." I supposed there were few enough folk left in the world now that when Gospel and I fell to it that would be a war, but it wouldn't really count. "And what with all the plagues and sicknesses that came after the war, it was good we had the Ministers, because there weren't folk enough to take up the work of the Lord. We needed them." Or at least that's what I'd been told in my classes, with Gospel for a bit and with a boy named Thom who had been only a year older than me but died of red sickness. After that there weren't any more classes at all, and besides, I'd had Mama to take care of by then too.

Auntie flexed her neck, bending her head to the left and the right. "So it's been the same Minister here the whole time?"

"Yes, ma'am. One of the oldest, one of the first made things. Once I saw a newer one, and it was fancy as could be, not worn out and threadbare like ours. I must've been only about four or so. That was the last time we saw more than a tinker in town." And there was something else, something I didn't mention because I had decided I was saying too much already. That other Minister, the fine and fancy one, I could remember that it had nodded its fine and fancy head at our Minister, what sat on our porch and didn't nod back at all, like it didn't have to.

"Your Ministers were up to something—they were all parts of the same great machine making bad things occur—what you see now as the fog, the cold, all of it. I could tell that much from my world. And I'm beginning to suspect that your exact Minister is the primary driver for it. The device that makes it all happen."

She was talking about things the same way Mama would have, back when she was carrying on her conversations with no one. And that's what finally made me start to believe the being in Mama's body. "Mama used to talk like you sometimes. She'd talk about all sorts of things that didn't make a lick of sense. I think she must have been saying what you were saying over there," I said, gesturing vaguely because I didn't really understand where the other world was. Of course, I couldn't really say where Heaven and Hell were neither, but that didn't make them less real.

"You poor girl, having to deal with that." The right leg drew up, her knee raising and then lowering, and the left a moment after as she continued speaking. "You're strong, Merciful, stronger than she was—Rebekkah, I mean. I tried to help her, but I didn't know what to do. Such strange times . . ." She closed her eyes and fell silent, and I wondered if she was gone again, or if she'd died for really real.

"Hello? Auntie?"

"I'm still here. Just thinking. Have you ever heard the phrase 'The first shall be the last'?" she asked, in a sort of way that made me know she was quoting, like from the Good Book. It *was* something the Minister had said, more than once, only I didn't know why or what it had meant, but now . . .

"You think it's the very first of them, because it's the very last?"

The eyes opened, shining white now, and the head nodded slowly. "The only one left, and it's bringing the world, every possible world, to an end. If we destroy it, it'll all stop. At least, your mother thought so."

Oh, how Mama had raged against the Minister in those last days of her decline, and now I guessed I knew why. "But how can we destroy it?"

"I don't know," Auntie said. "But it will not want you to. And it's powerful. More than I guessed."

I realized I was a stupid little girl, and Gospel was out in the snow because of me, and he'd never catch the Minister because it was terrible and clever and Heaven knows what all else. I didn't know what to say. I couldn't ever, I guessed, know what to say to Auntie. She weren't like anything else I'd ever seen, and there was no fashion in which she could be made familiar. And what she said . . . well, Gospel had the right of it in some way, 'cause it was unbelievable and seemed like a lie, but then again so was the cold unbelievable, the cold that was so intense that even in the cellar, where it should've been warmer, I could see every tiny breath I let out, and I was shaking on the steps, and even Auntie in Mama's dead body was giving off the faintest steam of heat in the frigid air.

I heard something upstairs and wondered if it was

Miz Cally up and moving. Or maybe Gospel had come back, and that was something I truly hoped for. But like a cloud came the thought that maybe it was neither of them. If it wasn't, that would be . . . well, it didn't bear thinking on at all.

Sixteen

I SCRAMBLED UP THE STAIRS, NOT CASTING ONE SINGLE look back at the thing at the bottom, and ran into the kitchen. The Widow was standing up, swaying like a willow tree with one ringed hand on the table and the other held to her head, where her hat had slipped and her smooth dark head shone in the light.

"Miz Cally, you're awake," I said, slipping my shoulder under her arm to help her stand.

"What's happened, girl? And why's it so blasted cold now?"

"I don't rightly know what happened, Miz Cally. The Minister, I think it did something to you. It made you go to sleep, or something like that." Really I kind of thought it had tried to kill her, but I didn't ought to say that, I guessed. A body didn't like to be told that something she had trusted for a span of years tried to push her into an early grave, and maybe that wasn't what happened at all, though not if you asked me. "Why it's cold . . . well, it's just been getting colder all this time, and the door's been opened for a moment and let out the warm." It sounded really stupid to say it like that, but it was the truth.

"For how long did I swoon?"

"An hour, or two hours, maybe. I don't rightly know. It's been cold and awful, and Gospel's gone out to chase the Minister, who ran away after it hurt you, and downstairs . . ." I fell silent.

She stood up on her own, looking down at me from her great height. "Downstairs what, Merciful? What's downstairs? Is there really some kind of horrible demon possessing your mama's poor unburied body? Tell me the truth, now, girl."

"The truth is there's something in there, and I don't know if it's good or if it's bad."

"You ain't been down there to speak with it, have you?"

I squirmed under her glance, and I didn't want to say I had. I knew I was probably trucking with the Devil when I talked to Auntie, and Miz Cally took all that sort of thing very seriously. So I didn't make a peep, which meant that of course she just pushed right past me, a little unstable still, and moved over to the stairs. The light in the cellar was dim and shaky, the oil in the lamp probably running low, but you could see something down there, a shifting something that was probably Mama's leg. The Widow set her hand on the hatch and flipped it down so that it closed with a bang.

"You will tell me right this instant what is happening down in the cellar, or so help me God I will turn you over my knee until you squeal out the truth. I expect it's something dreadful, just from the bit I could see, and I want to be prepared before I go to clean up that awfulness."

"You can't!" I wailed. I knew she meant to set herself to doing something, and the way that she talked back at her house maybe she knew well enough what needed doing. Which would be a sore trial if she got rid of Auntie, because I still thought we needed her, no matter how awful she was. "It's a lady who knew Mama. And Miz Cally, she's helping us."

"Helping you? Oh, no, child. That's possession, and that's a devil down there in the body, making it stir and move. If the Minister was here, we'd have an exorcism right now, no matter what you think that made thing might have done to me. But since it's gone, and probably not eager to come back, I gather, I'll have to do my part."

"Miz Cally, she knows things. Things that can help us, things that can stop the fog."

"We should rather be dead and saved than live and be damned, girl, and that's the sort of thing this'll lead to. Such a thing hasn't happened much since we got the Ministers, but it's the end of days, and all the heavens and hells are breaking loose, I expect. Now, are you going to help me or slow me down?" She tapped her foot expectantly.

I didn't know what to say, because I knew she was

mostly right—that it was something awful, whatever was inside Mama's body. On the other hand, I didn't want the world to end, and me still just a girl. So I clamped my mouth shut, and the Widow did just what she'd done before, which was ignore me being useless and get on with her business. In this case, she took up the bucket and the cloths that sat by the sink, picking them up for what reason I couldn't begin to guess, and she pulled open the cellar door.

Mama was right there, as if she had been waiting for the chance to make an entrance. She rose up, pushing from the stairs, and I screamed in surprise and a little in terror because she was awful bad to see in better light, all purple on her whole back half, and with a few spots where her skin was broken and weeping clear fluid, with her mouth hanging open and her eyes as pale as the storm outside. Esmeralda Cally, always practical, didn't scream at all, just swung the bucket of water overhand and brought it down, splashing like a fountain, on Mama's head. The whole operation produced a noise like a frog jumping into a pond, and then Auntie reeled back and tumbled down the stairs. With her other hand, the Widow flipped down the hatch and put one big boot right on top of it.

"That was plenty satisfying, indeed it was," the Widow said, and as she turned to look at me I dropped the hand that had risen to my mouth in fear. "Now, was that what you expected, Merciful?"

"No, ma'am."

"And did that seem friendly, and at all like your mama?"

"No, ma'am." I could hear something moving about in the cellar, the thump of something settling on the stairs and then a wheezing sound, and scraping. She was crawling up the stairs, I supposed, dragging herself maybe.

"Now do you see why I say we need to dispose of this thing?"

"Yes, Miz Cally."

"Then fetch me some snow, and we'll get to work on the matter."

I took the bucket from her hand where she held it out. "What do you need snow for?" I asked, because it was mighty cold outside and I didn't want to open the door.

"You can't cast out a spirit without pure water, girl, and snow's as pure as you'll get."

I was about to ask her why she didn't just get it herself seeing how the door was just three feet off from her, but then I took a moment and saw as how she was shuddering like a new chick. She was an old lady, after all, and probably this wasn't what she'd expected to do with her day. So I stepped over to the back door and opened it enough to scoop in a mound of snow, most of which ended up in the bucket, but some scattered on the wood of the kitchen floor. The thumping, scraping, and wheezing wafted yet from the cellar, but it sounded a little closer, and after I shut the door tight I hurried to carry the bucket back to the Widow's still-extended hand.

"Good work, girl. Now, it would be better if it was water proper, because water is cleansing, but there's enough good in snow, I suppose, and we ain't got no time to melt it down. And we ain't got a Minister to lead the prayers, but I might know them well enough, I guess, after a lifetime of praying."

"Wait," we could hear, muffled by the wood, "listen to me." Scratching and scraping, the body was climbing up closer, I could tell.

"Evil spirits don't impress me much. Open up that hatch, Merciful," the Widow said, and hefted the bucket up high as she started to pray for strength from the Lord. I lifted up the hatch and crouched by the back door, holding it up. Miz Cally was at the other end, where the stairs met the floor, while I was looking down into the dimness.

Auntie was draped across most of the steps, her head just a couple of stairs down from the opening. "I'm not an evil spirit," she croaked out. "I'm a woman, like you. I know you, Esmie. I know you inside and out."

"You don't have no right to call me by that name," the Widow said, and dumped down the mound of snow onto Mama's body, which was pulling itself bit by bit up the stairs.

"I've got all the right in the world. I know you, Esmie,

I know your sorrows," Auntie said. The snow hadn't seemed to hurt her none, and the Widow wasn't praying too steady, what with stopping to yell down at the thing in Mama's body.

"Don't tell me none of your lies," Miz Cally said, and then called on the Lord and started up her praying again.

I didn't think this was how an exorcism was supposed to go, with all the interruptions and the bickering, and if it hadn't been so generally terrifying, I suspected I might've laughed. But the one bloated hand that slapped down on the kitchen floor wasn't funny, and then the other reached out for the far edge of the flipped-up hatch and they both started to tug. Lurching, dripping wet, and with snow still piled on her back, Auntie loomed up into the kitchen. The Widow had stepped away. I could hear her praying up a storm, calling on the Good Lord to make it right.

The beast on the stairs pushed itself up, dragging its legs behind it, while the Widow stepped back farther, her hands making the sign of the cross. I crouched back against the kitchen door, feeling the cold of outside burning into me. Auntie straightened up fully and set her left leg onto the wood floor of the room. As she stepped out I could see that one leg didn't hold her straight at all, because it looked like it was broken in the calf, and I supposed that happened when she got knocked down. But if it was broke, it didn't stop her from standing on it. She listed just a bit to the right.

"Now, Esmie, you have two choices. You can keep pushing me down these stairs until you get tired of it and lock me in, though that won't keep me out of the way for long; or you can talk to me, the same as Merciful has, and see that while I look a bit ugly, I'm still a person. We don't have much time, only a few hours to talk, and then one way or another it'll all be over." Her hands were out before her like she was pleading.

There was something in her voice when she said the last bit. It was hard to tell, because she sounded dreadful all the time, but right then it seemed like there was even more dreadfulness, and it sent a shudder right down my spine. I bent my head down a little so I couldn't barely see, but I still peeked out through my eyelashes.

"Before all the saints and angels, I'll have no truck with you. Good Lord give me strength!" the Widow said. She snatched a necklace from around her neck, one with a big and dangling crucifix, and leaning forward she shoved hard at the thing's chest. I was mighty proud of her just then, for standing up for herself. Talking to the thing in Mama didn't seem like the best of notions anymore.

But Auntie didn't fall down this time. Instead those pleading hands reached up and wrapped around Miz Cally's wrists. The monster spun out of the way, pushing Miz Cally. I gasped as the old lady kept going forward, though I don't think she really much wanted to. She was moving fast, though, and was getting a bit of help from

Auntie, and before I could say anything, before I could do more than try to catch at her tall, falling form, she was taking a tumble down those stairs. The cellar door slammed shut behind her, bouncing off my knuckles as it passed. Auntie's half-purple, half-white hand had flipped it shut, and there was me with my hands outstretched only three feet from her, the skin scraped from the banging hatch. The fat hand reached up and pushed at her cheeks with spread fingers, twisting up the corners of her mouth, or trying to, so that she could make herself smile. Her lips split while she was doing it, and I felt like being sick again.

"I do believe I'm getting the hang of this body. Now, I've a few things to say, Merciful, and I expect you to listen carefully."

SEVENTEEN

THERE WAS A MOMENT OF SILENCE THEN, AND I STRAINED for any sound, even a groan, coming from the cellar, but there weren't nothing I could hear over the wind that still howled outside. I wondered if Gospel might suddenly come back and save me from what I'd got myself into, but I didn't figure that was very likely. No, not very likely at all. He'd been gone awhile now, though I wasn't sure exactly how long. It was so cold inside that even with the fires going the snow had barely melted inside the back door and my breath was a visible fog every time I panted out my fear, so that I couldn't think he'd be all right outside. I was sorely sad that I had sent my only family out into the horrible wilds. Didn't suppose it much mattered, though, as we weren't likely to get to make up with each other.

I did about the only thing I could, which was to shuffle my feet around the cellar door real slow and hope she didn't notice I was moving until I was out of her reach.

After all, her eyes were milky and rotten, and I thought she probably didn't see none too good. Except she had seen the Widow without any problem, when she needed to. Whatever this thing was, she wasn't quite what she had tried to seem in the basement, helpless and confused. After I figured I was far enough from her grip, I spun on my heel and bolted away with the quickness that only a girl with an older brother can muster. Around the table and through the door I went, into the god-awful sitting room, which was frigid cold and covered in the blood of that danged hen that lay by the door, dead in a pool of slick, frozen red.

With the hatchet propped by the door where Gospel had left it, shining and bloody.

I heard the creak of the floor behind me and knew she was moving, but I didn't guess how fast. Long steps, too long for the way she looked, too long even for Mama's height, and I reached down for the hatchet and took it in my mittened hand and realized that was no way to hold it, because it would just slip loose—but I didn't have time. Both hands around it, I turned, and there she was. She stood up above me like a mountain, so tall. I was always a little afraid of Mama when she was alive, she was so big a lady, and not afraid to hit a body either, but this was different. Auntie seemed even taller, and I could tell there was a fierce strength in her. She wasn't putting on a show anymore, she was being true, and I didn't know if there was anything a girl could do against her, but I had to try. And by this time I was pretty certain there was just selfishness and wickedness in there, but I still wasn't sure that maybe she didn't know something we could use all the same. I just couldn't tell no more.

She looked terrible, but she didn't actually do anything. She stared and glared, and I held the hatchet in my mittens and panted, and then she stepped back.

"You don't trust me any longer," she said.

"No, ma'am, that I do not."

"I've only tried to help. I'm sorry about Esmie. I know her so well from all the care and attention she showed your mother that I feel like I'm her friend, and it's a shame what had to be done. She has a strong will, and she wouldn't listen. I do hope she's not hurt too badly. I understand how you wouldn't trust me. But if you don't listen to me, this world will be gone. Her injury, her death, won't mean a thing. That will be your fault if you haven't tried to help. Our time is running short."

I didn't want to listen. I just wanted to go and help Miz Cally, and wait for Gospel, and then maybe if the world ended, it wouldn't be so bad, because at least I'd be able to apologize to him for being a stupid little girl. But on the other hand, I didn't want to die. I didn't want the fog to get me. And probably Auntie knew how to stop that from happening. So I guessed I would listen, but I'd listen to her like she was Mama toward the end, when she was plumb crazy and you had to be careful with doing anything she wanted you to. Because this angel, this devil, this thing in my mama's body, was just as mad as Mama.

I didn't put down the hatchet, but I didn't hit her either. "What do you got to say?"

"I haven't been as honest with you as I could have been. I know more than I've said."

"Well I hope so, or whatever plan you got ain't got a chance."

"It only has a chance with you, Merciful. Only if you do as I say."

"The first thing we got to do is help Miz Cally."

The thing looked like it was ready to spit for just a second before it put that face away, and I stepped back but then she got all calm again. "All right, but I can't help you. My hands don't work very well for anything delicate." She balled them up into rough fists, and I could tell she didn't mean that just for show. "You can see to her, if you like. I'll have a seat in the rocker and wait for you." She slipped around the chairs, her dead eyes not leaving me, and I kept a watch on her all the way to the bedroom door. Not that I thought I could stop her if she tried to do something, but I at least wanted to know where she was. I ran into the kitchen, tossing the hatchet onto the table, and dropped to my knees to pull up the cellar door. There was no light at all at the bottom, so I couldn't see anything.

"Miz Cally?" I called down. "Miz Cally?"

Something stirred in the darkness.

"Miz Cally?" I whispered.

"Hello, little girl," a voice said, a voice that was as if the Widow had tried to sound like a man. I moaned with a sudden dire fear, fear so strong it made everything that had come before seem like a bedtime story. "Looks like someone left open the door for me."

I reached out and slammed the hatch down hard. The big chair was only a few feet away, and I moved it right on top, and then the smaller chairs too, and the bucket. I didn't expect it'd do much, but whatever was down there wasn't the Widow Cally anymore, and it made the thing on the rocker seem just about comforting. Even with the door shut, even with things piled on it, I still felt the evil coming from the cellar.

Somewhere inside the wailing wind and my panting breath I thought I heard something. Faint and weak, like a scratch on the door.

Gospel.

Crawling to the back door, I pulled myself to my feet holding on to the handle. I could tell now that the scratching was definitely there, that it wasn't just my mind, too tired and worn, making things up. It had to be Gospel, weak from the cold.

Only it wasn't. When I opened the door, a squirrel rested on the mounded snow without leaving the faintest impression. It was the Minister, bushy little tail held over its tiny head like an umbrella, all the fur on its underside draggled and wet.

It sprang in past me and was gone just as quick. I couldn't see it anywhere in the kitchen, but then, it wasn't too bright in the room anymore, just one lamp lit and the glow from the stove and a single candle on the table. I looked outside but didn't see any sign of my brother.

"Where's Gospel, Minister?"

"He is outside." The Minister's voice came echoing from everywhere and nowhere.

"You left him out there?" I sent my eyes around in the dim, looking for any sign of the little made thing.

"He was angry, Merciful. He would have hurt me if he had found me. I made certain he didn't find me and came back as soon as I could."

"He's going to die out there!"

"It is likely, yes."

"You have to go and find him, lead him back. He won't be able to hurt you if he's freezing." I didn't mean to sound as desperate as I did, but I couldn't help it. Even if he wasn't any good at it, Gospel was my only brother.

"Perhaps not, but the fog you two spoke of has come closer. I don't dare get too close to that fog, Merciful. The consequences would be terrible."

"I don't care, Minister. You get on out there and you bring him back, right now! I know what you are now, you dang blasted machine, so you just make yourself into something that can rescue him and you go find my brother!"

"Ah," it said, that and nothing more for a long moment. "Merciful," the calm voice continued, still without any source I could place. It seemed sad to me, sad and weary. "You don't understand enough."

A creaking and then a smash came from the cellar. I thought I could see something start in the shadows on top of one of the cabinets. I can't claim I didn't jump a little too.

"What was that?" the Minister asked. "I feel I should know, but I have been . . . distracted."

"I don't rightly know."

"Is your mother's body still down there?"

"Not anymore. What's down there is worse," I said. I had crept over to the cabinet, and now I gave it a shake. The Minister sprang light as the wind from there to the table, and then away with me in pursuit, trying to get my hands around its tail.

We both pulled up short at the end of the table. Standing in the doorway was Auntie, and she didn't look the least unhappy to see the Minister. Just the opposite, really. That smile was back on her face, and I didn't like it one bit.

Eighteen

"Minister," auntie said gently. the minister's body twitched from head to tail, and I reached for that tail with my right hand, again thinking about how bad a mitten was for holding things. If she could keep him distracted for another moment, I thought I might get the dang thing off, and started to do it, taking the knit tip into my mouth and grabbing it with my teeth. "I've been wondering where you got off to. Did you bring back Gospel as well?"

The Minister didn't say a thing, and my hand was moving back toward its tail, which stood up like scotch broom, the fur flared out wild-like. I could tell it was more terrified even than me.

"I gather you didn't. Well, I'd rather have both of them just in case, but Merciful will still do by herself. Now come here!" she said, and lunged forward. Her hands, like she'd said, weren't working good. The fingers were all swelled up and puffy, and it didn't look like she could get a grip on anything, even less than me in the mittens. But that didn't matter, because *her* moving set the Minister to moving, and I closed my frosty hand on nothing at all as it sprang away onto the counter on the back wall and then bounded back toward the door. "Get it, girl, get it!"

"Do not trust this thing, Merciful," the Minister said, bounding across the chairs that were on the cellar door. "It lies and lies and lies yet more."

"I ain't doin' it for her, Minister. You got to tell me what you know about how to stop all this nonsense!"

"A liar, am I?" Auntie said, stepping into the kitchen. "We'll see where the lies are and whether there isn't truth worse than a lie, won't we, Minister?" She was headed toward the stove, and I was following the Minister's path, so that we accidentally had both sides of the table covered. I was pretty glad to have the table between us, because I surely didn't feel like Auntie had any good feelings for me by now, and it was mutual. The Minister was perched waiting on the back of the big chair with one tiny paw held up, the body about to spring. Toward what I didn't know. But the little made thing was caught.

"Come to me, Minister," I said.

"Yes, go to her," Auntie said, the ends of her mouth still twisting up like it was supposed to be a smile, like it didn't matter whether she or I ended up with the Minister.

The squirrel looked from her to me. "I will not."

Then the chair jerked. There was a thump from below, and I stopped moving at once, because I knew what it was. Miz Cally, or whatever was in her, was trying to get loose, and the chairs and such wouldn't keep it still for long, I knew that much.

"Let me out of here," the strange man voice of the Widow's body bellowed from below.

Auntie's reaction startled me, for Mama's body drew back and seemed to fall into itself a little, looking smaller than she had in life, even in the last days when she lay still and barely moved at all. "He can't be here," she said real soft.

I was about to ask her who she meant, but right then the Minister made its move, and neither of us could do a thing to stop it. It right about flew to the kitchen table, a great huge leap for such a small thing and with so little buildup, but, squirrels did all sorts of things that I couldn't never account for. Of course, I knew by then it wasn't just a squirrel, even if my fool mind was still attempting to suggest that idea to me over and over. I tried to grab the Minister but just ended up sprawled on the table, knocking the hatchet aside as the made thing bounded away and into the sitting room. I wanted to follow it there for sure and certain, and let the things in the two tall women deal with each other. That kitchen wasn't a place for a girl like me, and so my hand found the hatchet just in case, and I scooted away. Not too quick, so as not to attract Auntie's attention.

She didn't even glance at me as I crept away into the sitting room, where the cold was like a barefoot walk out to get eggs, and I wished for my mitten back on my hand, though the hatchet felt kind of good there too. I could hear the thumps of something hitting the hatch over and over, not so hard or heavy as to get out, but solid and steady. I wondered if whatever was down there didn't want to get out just yet, or if it was too weak still, the way Auntie had been for a little bit, when she'd been stretching and flexing while I talked to her. And if it was yet too weak, could Auntie defeat it?

"Minister?" I called out as I moved farther into the sitting room. I guess I weren't too surprised when it didn't answer. I mean, there's me with a hatchet in my hand creeping into a dark room, calling for something I've been trying to catch for a time, and it'd have to be stupid to answer me. The Minister wasn't stupid.

"Minister, I just want to know where Gospel could be. Do you know where he's at? If you won't go out there, I got to go and get him, and you're the only one who knows anything."

The chairs were only shadows, and the floor was slick with blood that felt like it had frozen over. I had to move careful to get across and come to the bedroom, where the air was a little warmer, a little better, and where there was a little light. I could see the Minister, reared up with its tail high, perched on the edge of the bed, with the faint glow of coals casting a ruddy light. The fire had died long ago.

"He's near the barn," the Minister said. "Build up the fire before you go to look for him."

"If I bring him back, those things in the kitchen will probably just kill us both."

If it could shrug, it did. "I can't say for certain. They are alien to me. Outside my experience, outside the Good Lord's intentions. I do not know what they might do. But I fear the worst, yes."

I swallowed hard, but I did what it said and went to build up the fire. The thumps were still audible, but I tried not to pay any attention to them, though each one made me jump a little. My hands were shaking, and not just from the cold of the house.

"What are those things? The one says it's Mama from another place, and the other . . . well, it felt like a devil, just hearing it talk."

"They aren't meant to be here, not in this world. Both of them are like dreams, like God's nightmares. They shouldn't exist, and yet they do. The closing of the world is upon us, and the Lord is at work on His tasks. The rules are bending, breaking. Otherwise, they wouldn't be here."

"What rules?"

"God's rules, child. The ones that I am here to

enforce, as best I can, though I've precious little strength for my tasks now. Still, I am a Minister of Grace, shaping the world to make it better, holier, more suited for the Lord." It sounded like normal Minister talk, but I had never heard this line before, never in all the days of my life. I wondered if this was what Auntie had been talking about, because those words made it sound like the Minister was certainly changing things, making the world different. Destroying it, but maybe to save it? Like Miz Cally did to herself when she tried to fight against Auntie.

"Can you make them go away? Miz Cally said you could do an exorcism to get rid of them."

"An exorcism?" It laughed, which was a thing it almost never did. This was bitter and mocking. "At another time, in another place, surely I could do that. Even you could've done it. But not now, no. Not now." Which was disappointing, but not terribly surprising. The Minister hadn't been good for much lately, worn-out old made thing that it was.

But I had to concentrate on Gospel. "How cold is it outside?"

"As cold almost as ever it will be. Cold enough that if your face is uncovered, you'll be frostbit in moments. Wrap a scarf around, carefully, and move as quickly as you can."

I wished for my other mitten, but it was back in the kitchen, far beyond any chance of my fetching it. I went to the stacks of clothes I had sorted out and gathered up a scarf, a long old thing Mama had loved but that I couldn't stand, with daisies and such stitched into it, and I wound it around my head again and again. I grabbed a blanket from my bed and wrapped it around me, because it was the only thing large enough to cover up Mama's big coat. I was almost kind of warm for a minute, with the fire roaring and the layers all around me, and my breath toasty on my wrapped face.

The hatchet I set by the bedroom door; it wouldn't be any good to me outside. "Can you do anything at all to stop those things in the kitchen?" I asked.

There was a long silence. "Go find Gospel," the Minister finally said, and I had to be satisfied with that for an answer. I turned to go.

"God go with you, Merciful, and bless you and keep you," the Minister said, soft and gentle like it always tried to be. For a moment it was like I was a young girl again, because I felt as if the Minister's blessing really did mean something. I stood a little taller, seemed a little warmer, just for that moment. It stared at me with worried, wet black eyes, and I realized that whatever else it was, whatever it was doing, it was good in its soul, if a machine could have one.

I nodded to the small made thing and walked to the front door, trying not to notice that the thumping had gotten louder. A looming shadow showed Mama's body still stood in the kitchen, the lamplight picking it out.

What I guessed was the biggest kitchen knife was loosely clamped in Auntie's swollen hands. She was standing just by the cellar door, swaying slightly, her shadow shifting eerily. "James, what are you doing here?" she said, softly, not like she was asking anyone. Who was James? The devil down in Miz Cally? I decided I didn't really want to know. I needed to get to Gospel.

I crept across the bloody floorboards of the sitting room, wincing every time they squeaked, but outside the wind howled and I don't expect Auntie heard me moving around at all.

It didn't much matter; I'd have done it anyways. I was all the family Gospel had, and I had to go find him. When we got back, we'd deal with Auntie and the thing in the Widow and the Minister. We'd figure something out together.

I wished I could've gone by the back door, because the trek would have been so much shorter. There was no way to do it, though, with Auntie right there and whatever it was in the cellar just waiting to come on out once it got strong enough. Cold as it was, I'd have to push around the house.

I opened the door.

Nineteen

I NEVER FELT NO COLD AS BAD AS WHEN I OPENED THAT door and the hard wind slapped my face as if I'd been the worst little girl in the world. It was like a fist, like a hammer, like the absolute horriblest feeling in the world, and it made me gasp and fall back a step and think about curling up under quilts by the fire and just waiting for the end. But I didn't do that. I sorely wanted to, but I didn't. Instead I pushed out the door, then struggled to pull it shut behind me, and wondered how it had got so cold inside my coats and scarves and all that when just a minute ago I had been warm. Didn't a body make at least *some* heat?

There was snow hurtling down from the sky, wicked thick snow with huge flakes that were settling on the deep piles already on the ground. And even on the front porch, where there was an eave and some shelter, the white stuff was inches deep. I couldn't even see the stairs down to the yard, because they were completely covered, and I could see only hints that Gospel had been out, not an hour ago, after the Minister.

The snow wasn't so bad to move through, at least. It was deep and dense, but while I was clumsy in it, there was a sort of ground beneath my feet. And there wasn't any ice, which I felt was lucky, because one fall and I might be done for. But it was a long trip around the house to the barn.

That cold cut into a body, and it made me ache like I knew the Widow had ached from her rheumatism, and me a girl just twelve years of age. But it was *that* cold, and my body was shuddering and shivering all at once, and making me want nothing more than to keep moving right on back into the house, which I wasn't about to do. I thought about calling Gospel's name as I rounded the corner of the house, past the kitchen windows, where there was a faint glow through the frost, but I couldn't even hear myself the first time I tried. The wind was so strong and whooshing, I didn't give it no more effort, for the cold just snatched the warm from me every time I opened my mouth. I had precious little warm left to lose.

I was starting to stumble now in the high drifts that were piled against that side of the house. The wind was blowing from the north, and the kitchen was on the north face, and the snow was massing up into a slope that I didn't want to get lost in. It was dark, but not so dark as it could've been, with the faint shine of snow and so on, but if I hadn't known the house was right *there*, and the old tree was right *there*, and the barn had to be right *there*, then I would've been in for a terrible time indeed. Instead, I made it to the bare patch of snow that would be the garden in warmer times, and crossed it toward the barn. In the lee of the barn, hidden from the wind and the worst of the cold, I could just barely make out a set of tracks, more dimples in the snow, which I guessed must have been Gospel. I couldn't tell anymore which way they went, forward or back, but they went someplace, that was sure, and the Minister had said Gospel'd be out by the barn, so I pushed on.

I wouldn't have found him, I'm sure of it, except that I tripped over him. He was under the snow, under a layer like a coverlet, with his back propped up against the barn, so that once I could get a good look at him, I could see his head with barely any snow on it. He wasn't moving, and I couldn't even begin to tell if he was breathing or living at all, but it didn't matter. It was Gospel, and the Good Lord had brought me to him. I was so sore, though, and so tired already from pushing along in the wind and the cold, and I didn't know if I could drag my brother back to the front door. He was bigger than me, even if he wasn't as big as Miz Cally or Mama, and I guessed the back door would be the only choice, even as bad as that was like to be with the two things in there having a tussle.

But I grabbed his arm anyway, where I found it curled up on his chest after I dug for just a second, and I pulled and tugged and got him to flop forward, and then I struggled and strained and it seemed like I was going somewhere, only the snow kept shifting under me. My feet couldn't keep a place, and I kept falling, and after what seemed like an hour but couldn't have been more than a couple minutes I was exhausted, with snow leaking into my sleeves, and my scarf slipped and my face pretty much numb, and Gospel only a few feet from the barn and almost the whole of the garden still to be crossed, yards and yards of it ahead of me.

I couldn't do it. I started to cry, and felt that the tears were hardening on my face as soon as they left my eyes. Oh, Lord, I was lost and weak and feeble, and I didn't have any chance. So I prayed for a miracle and hoped that He'd hear me.

And then Gospel stirred. I would've thought he'd be dead to the world if he wasn't just plain dead, him out in the cold for so long, but he stirred, and he pushed up just a little, and I slipped down quick as a cat and got under his arm. Together we got him to his feet, and we stumbled on across that patch of snow that had my tracks all scattered along it, half-filled already from the storm, and we headed right for the back door with the tiny window that still shone like the last hope of Heaven.

I thought he was saying something the whole time we were walking, even if over the wind I couldn't make it out. Maybe it was words, or maybe just moaning or somesuch, but at least a bit of him was still working. The garden seemed enormous. We fell a time or two, and each time it was harder to get up, harder to pull Gospel up after me. The last time, we were just in front of the back door, just a few feet from the house, from a bit of warmth and light and life. So close, and I could barely get to my feet. Gospel lay there, facedown in the snow, so I just grabbed him and dragged again. The wind was fierce, the cold worse even than when I came out, though maybe that was just because I was chilled straight through to the bone. But he moved well enough, I suppose, between me pulling and his legs pushing back against the snow like he was swimming in it.

The door opened as we got there. There was a tall shape, wrapped in what looked like a big, heavy, tattered coat, and I didn't know which one it was. I guess it didn't matter, really, because we needed to get in, and if something awful happened there, at least we'd be in the warm when it did. The first touch of the house air felt like summer, and then hands were pulling me in, pulling Gospel in, and we collapsed in a snowy pile just inside the door.

No one was there when I looked up. The cellar hatch was open, the chairs tossed aside, and the table had been smashed in half, buckled right down the middle, with splinters to mark where it had given way. Whoever had helped us in had vanished as swift as a mouse, and as quiet. It seemed like I could hear every noise in the house, the tiny pops of the remains of fire in the stove, the faint breathing from Gospel, the sound of the rocker in the bedroom, and yet I hadn't heard a board creak or anything. Nothing was moving about except that slow squeaking from the bedroom, the chair rocking back and forth.

"Gospel?" I shook his shoulder and tried to turn him over, but I was spent. There was nothing left in me at all. He groaned, real faint, and then I couldn't do any more. I had saved him, or done what I could to save him. Maybe it was too late, but at least I had tried. I dropped down next to him, his freezing body starting to shake and spasm and jerk, and I wrapped my arms around him and put my cold face next to his, and I whispered in his ear, "I'm sorry" and "I love you" and all the things I should have said to him all the time and never did. How deep it seemed, what was between us two: deep as a well and as hard to see into, and maybe I was wrong about how I felt when I said I hated Gospel. Lord forgive me for a liar. Gospel was my brother, and somehow I loved him. I just wished he could love me back.

I was starting to shake too, my body trying so hard to soak up a little warmth that every muscle was atwitter, and I couldn't stop, couldn't even slow it down, but it didn't matter, it felt so warm inside, so very warm, and I felt like I could just drift off and let go. Even with the shakes, that's just what I did.

TWENTY

I WOKE UP THINKING IT WAS BREAKFAST TIME, WITH the smell of bread in the air and Mama singing like she did when I was a little girl, before everything went wrong. I felt warm and comfortable, and my head was pillowed on something soft and nice, and I wanted to go back to sleep and stay that way a little longer.

But I opened my eyes and pushed myself up and realized it *was* warm, or warmer, at least. The fire in the stove was burning bright, there was the bread loaf sliced and toasted up, and there was a steaming kettle set on the counter beside it, and two cups that steamed as well, as if someone had just been there setting things out for tea. The Minister was perched on the edge of the counter, by the cups, looking down at me with its little black eyes, nose twitching.

"You rested for a time," it said. "Not a long time."

"It's warm," I said. It was the first thing that came into my head. "Did you make it warm?"

"In a way, yes. The Good Lord works through me to preserve you."

The thing I had been lying on was Gospel's shoulder, my brother's face turned away as he lay on his belly on the floor. I rolled him over and almost started to cry. He looked dead, his nose and cheeks blackened and dry, his face other than that pale and ghostly. But I could tell he was breathing, feel his chest swelling and sinking, and then I did start to cry. "You're alive," I whispered.

"He is, though it was a near thing," the Minister said. "I was able to help him, and you. I don't expect you'll even have frostbite, but it was as good as I could do for him to make it less than it was."

"Thank you."

"No gratitude to me is needed. The work is the Good Lord's, and it is Him you should thank. And pray to Him, because we have very little time."

I stared at my brother for a moment longer and then rolled over to look at the Minister. "Is it over?"

A tiny shrug. "The two abominations are almost done with their parley. Soon they will either fight again or unite. Either way, I expect we'll all be in trouble." I didn't like to hear the Minister sounding so concerned about things. Sickness, death, the end of the world—in fact, nothing had ever in my life made it bothered much. But these two tall women and the things that were in them had it bothered. I couldn't hardly think of how bad they must be.

"They fought already?" The smashed table, the tossed chairs. They had to have.

"They fought, yes. Like demons, like mad dogs. But at the same time . . . I can't say for certain that their bodies fought at all. Their souls fought, that much I could feel." It bent low over its paws and shivered. "A grim battle to perceive, wicked and bitter. They struggled that way, and maybe their bodies did as well. *Something* broke the table. After a time, a minute and no more probably, they withdrew into the bedroom and have been talking, if you can call it that, since."

"What are they talking about?"

"I can only faintly hear them," it said, another surprise. The Minister's ears were sharp. "They speak in a way that doesn't really involve their mouths. Only a little, and that little I can hear. They know each other, these things: know each other well, it seems. They spoke of past offenses that the first one had made against the second, but then they stopped, and started to speak of me. The first one, it wants me to be destroyed. But you know that," it said with a faint air of accusation, and I looked down for a moment. "The second one wants instead to capture me. It wants to use me for . . . for things that you wouldn't understand. Things worse than you can imagine, gentle child that you are."

"I don't think there's anything worse than the world ending," I said.

"There is so much worse than that," the Minister

said, and its voice was softer even than normal, like when Gospel and I would talk during prayer time years ago, quiet and soft and trying not be heard. "The end of the world is meant to be, Merciful. It's part of the plan. Everything ends. But what that second thing wants . . . such a horror hasn't been conceived in a very long time. For the moment, the first thing opposes it, but this may not last."

"Then we have to get away," I said, though I dreaded returning to the snow. Whatever the Minister had done, to Gospel or Miz Cally or anyone, it hadn't killed them. And I could tell that the second thing, it wouldn't stop for an instant at killing someone. It was evil through and through.

"I can't go out again. It's too close to the end, the fog is too near. I mustn't come into contact with it. And as for *you*, the cold is getting even worse, the storm more fierce. You and your brother wouldn't survive even as long as you did last time. No, we have to stay. And you have to decide what you'll do."

"Me? What do I matter?"

"You and Gospel, you're the only human beings left in all of God's creation. You matter more than you can know. The fate of the world could turn on what you decide." It shivered my spine when the Minister said that.

"Decide about what?"

"About me. Whether you try to save me or kill me or help capture me. Whether you oppose those things or split their partnership or hide from them or help them.

Whether you stand aside or take action. Everything you do from now on is a decision, and every decision will matter. Even now, God's will might not be unbending, His choices not undeniable." It hopped back a foot or so to put itself behind one of the cups, and setting its tiny paws on one, pushed it almost right to the edge of the counter. "Drink your tea—it's the last in the world, and there won't be any more. It will warm you better and longer than I have."

I reached for the mug and took it in my hands, one still in a mitten that was damp but not soaked like it should have been from all the snow. The Minister had done a lot more than it let on. The cup was almost too hot, even through the wool, but I loved the warm on my fingers, which still felt a little chilled, and the way the steam curled up in my face. Gospel gave a little sigh beside me and smacked his lips, and I could tell he was starting to wake up. I blew on the tea and wondered how the little Minister had gotten down the cups, heated up the water, poured: all that it had done. And I remembered the tall, strong figure in the door, the one I couldn't make out. The Minister was a changing machine, I knew that now even if I half forgot it when I didn't think on it, and I wondered if it could be more than a squirrel, better than a dog or a cat.

"Do you ever look different?" I asked, with the steam around my face because the cup was right under my chin.

The Minister twitched and then became absolutely

still. The dark eyes were fixed on me. I thought it was nervous, but not scared like it had been so many times in the last two days. Finally, the tiny head bobbed once, real fast, and then went still again.

"Did you open the door for us?" I already knew the answer, but I wanted it to tell me.

"I must care for you, spiritually and physically," the little creature said, and scrunched down into itself, back arched, paws forward, much of its little face hidden.

"Why can't I tell? Why don't I notice? Why do I only sort of remember, even after I know it's happened?"

"You aren't meant to. You shouldn't even be able to ask me that question, but . . . the end of days is coming. Everything is breaking down. I have few secrets left, and fewer will remain before the end."

Gospel drew in breath real sudden like, and jerked up with his eyes wide and his hands clenching in their gloves. "I'm cold," he said.

"You're fine. The Minister helped you." I passed him my cup, which I hadn't even drunk from yet. He looked at me out of tired eyes, with those scabby black patches on his nose and chin, and his lips chapped and dry, and I wished I had never let him go out. He held to that cup like a treasure, and I reached up for the other mug, and we sat there a moment in the closest thing to quiet for a while.

"I'm sorry," I said after a minute. "Sorry you had to go outside because I'm a stupid, willful child."

Gospel glugged down some tea and then shook his

head. "Nah, you ain't stupid, and no more willful than I am. I'm the one as should be sorry, making you deal with all this deviltry."

I set down the cup, and I leaned over and wrapped one arm around him. It felt weird, hugging my brother, and I guessed it must have felt really strange for him, too. He patted my back twice with his free hand, and then gently he pushed me away and took up my cup and put it back in my hand.

A long, quiet moment passed as we sipped our tea. Too quiet. The rocking had stopped.

"Minister? Are they still talking?"

"They who?" Gospel said.

"Auntie, and somebody worse than her. I'll tell you in a minute. Minister?"

"No. They've stopped."

We heard the creaking of the floor, one set of steps and then another coming toward us from the far end of the house. Gospel pushed up from the floor and then slumped back down, his cup spilling brown tea all over the floor. The Minister sprang away, into shadows and darkness, and left us behind.

From the darkness of the sitting room came a thick and bubbly voice. "Hush, my babies, don't you cry." And then a deeper chuckle.

I could stand, I knew it. I could stand and be ready for them. But instead I just pressed back against Gospel, who took my hand, and we waited.

TWENTY~ONE

"WHERE IS THE MINISTER?" THE DEEP VOICE SAID. The tall black woman stepped into the room, her neck bent all the way to the side so that her head sat heavily on her shoulder, and I screamed a tight little scream that cut off because my voice froze up. Gospel moaned behind me. There were still rings on the fingers, those long, dark fingers that were bent a little with age but otherwise had been so clever. Auntie followed a few steps behind, Mama going bad right in front of us. Her face was soft and doughy, sagging down and splitting like a badly baked cake.

"Lord God Almighty, what the Hell are you?" Gospel yelped, his voice shaking a little.

"An old . . . friend of Rebekkah's who's come to call. Now where is our little Minister?"

"It went away," Gospel said, soft now behind my ear.

"Where did it go?" The lips on that sideways head moved as the devil spoke, which was awful, just awful, to see. The eyes were open and didn't ever blink, and the face never moved at all except for the lips, not a twitch.

"We don't know," I said, and I was honest and sounded it. I didn't know where it had gone, no better than they did, so I surely wasn't lying. The two horrors circled closer, each of them moving one slow foot in front of the other. They looked like mirrors of one another, both so tall, the one bald and with rings all over her hands, the other with long hair and bare, rotting fingers, each one sliding a foot forward and then following with the body. So slow they moved, and so terrible. My eyes went from the one to the other, and I didn't see any hint that they meant the least bit of good.

"What are you?" Gospel asked again, his voice thin and high, cracking like it almost never did anymore.

They stopped and looked at each other. Auntie nodded her head a little and stepped back just a half pace, sliding away the same as she had forward. The other one smiled a little sideways smile. "We are," she said, her man voice strange in Miz Cally's mouth, "the last of our world. The same as you. My companion is a scientist where we come from, and she discovered the doorway into this world." There was something more that it wasn't telling us. It knew something about how Auntie had come here, for certain. "And she was *able* to come here because a part of her was here already, as I suppose she's told you. Me, well, I just took the opportunity, at the last instant. Followed her the way she'd come, you could say. The rules are changing."

It was so much like what the Minister had said that I thought it must be true.

"But what are you?"

"I'm a dark angel now, come to rid the world of all its troubles. And you're going to help me," it said. "Help me by finding the Minister. Or you could not help me, but then I'd get terribly angry."

And it reached up with both hands and gripped the frame of the cabinet that the Minister had hid on, not too long ago, and with one jerk tore it from the wall, to crash down on the broken table. Bits splintered off and showered Gospel and me. I think I let out a scream, but if I did, Gospel's was louder, and angrier, too. He jumped right up behind me, so that I kind of tumbled over without him to lean back against anymore. And then he grabbed up one of the legs of the table, that had broken almost all loose but with a chunk of wood still at the top, and he held it in both hands like he was getting ready to toss rocks and hit them. It was longer and probably more dangerous than his knife, but I didn't think it was good enough to get to those devils. I didn't know whether to laugh or cheer; mostly I wanted to tell him to sit down, because they would kill him. But they didn't.

No, the two of them stayed mostly where they were, only shifting a little to be sideways to Gospel. The Widow figure lowered its arms and stared from that side-cocked head without a smile at all now, and Auntie's swollen hands were clenched as best they could be and looked ready to hit something, but they didn't move. Neither did Gospel, for which I thanked the Lord above. I scrabbled behind him and to my feet. "What's the plan?" I asked in a whisper.

"I ain't got no plan, Merciful. We can't run, we can't hide no place. Maybe I can hurt one or both of these devils and that's good enough, right?"

"You don't want to hurt us," came Mama's scratchy, wet voice, a thing I can't rightly describe. It was still her, almost, but from a throat that didn't want to talk at all and barely could. "We're your only hope to live. The Minister won't leave you alive, you know."

"It's true. God is done with this world. He's going to end it. The Minister is His instrument, and when it ends, so will you. The Minister will let you die. But we can stop it." The Widow stepped a tiny bit closer, a pace far too small for the long, long legs under its skirts.

"You better stay back where you are." Gospel cocked back the table leg. I could see his arms shaking, but I hoped that maybe the two dead things couldn't tell as well as I could how weary my brother was.

"You don't understand," Auntie said. "This is the truth: the Minister is to blame. It's the machine I've told you about, changing itself and changing the world. The God it serves is done with both our worlds and wants them gone. But it's not too late to save them. To save everyone."

"Everyone?" I said.

Mama's poor dead head nodded. "We can save everyone, put everything back the way it was, if you just help me. Help me, Merciful," she said with the white eyes meeting mine, and for a moment she sounded just like my mama in those last desperate days when she finally knew something was wrong with her and couldn't make it right. My mama, begging me for help, and there hadn't been a thing I could do. Oh, how it hurt to hear that same painful plea from this monster, and how I ached to find a way to help whatever in her was left of the woman who birthed me. But I knew there wasn't even one bit of Mama actually in there.

"You have to kill the Minister," Auntie said.

"*No*," the other one said, cutting her off. "It's not to die, or we can't get *even*."

"I don't give a fig what either of you want," Gospel said. "We don't have the Minister, and we're not getting it for you. It's a waste to even ask. Get it yourself if you're so all-fired powerful. Do your own damned dirty work."

"I suppose I can afford to kill *one* of you . . ." The Widow's man voice drifted off, and it started forward, arms reaching out and seeming even longer than they ever had in life, the jewels on the rings shining in the light from the lamp and the stove's merry flame making long shadows on the wall, shadows that hid Auntie, who didn't move at all. If Gospel was scared, he didn't show it. He waited, waited for the arms to get close, and then he swung that table leg fast as he could, batting first one arm, then the other, away, and then leapt into the gap, the arms closing in on him fast, and brought the chunk of wood down on the Widow's already broken neck. The club came down hard, onto the dark soft skin of the old lady who had taught me how to play rummy and how to knit and how to make apple cider. Her neck split right open, and I let out one more scream as the head dropped away with a thump. The thing, whatever it was, reeled back and away, falling over. It was reaching out, legs jerking around.

I'd been clinging to Gospel's coat and had jumped forward with him, my hands slipping around his sides, until I felt something there and remembered the gun he always wore. It wasn't much use, of course, but the things wouldn't know that, would they? So when the Widow started to stand up again, I reached into my brother's big, baggy coat and pulled out the gun, while he turned to look at me with shock. I put my fingers on the trigger and lined it up with the old woman's chest. I just tried to pretend I hadn't known her, hadn't loved her. My friend was gone.

"You stop moving right now, whatever you are."

I don't know how I thought it could hear me or see what I was doing, without a head. But I wasn't surprised that it stopped in the middle of getting up, one hand on the floor pushing up, one knee down too, the other leg bent and one hand out, reaching toward Auntie. She still hadn't moved, like she was waiting for one of us to make a mistake. Waiting for her chance. Her head tilted now, a little, and the white eyes were on me, so I turned the gun on her.

"There aren't any bullets in that gun. Your mother got rid of them all after what happened."

"There are bullets," I said, but I knew there weren't. Mama hadn't let us keep any, because of how Papa got himself killed with thinking he could win a fight.

"No, Rebekkah threw them all away after your father shot himself."

"After . . . what do you mean?" The gun shook in my hand, all feeling gone from me. "Papa got shot by a stranger."

"Don't listen to that thing, Merce," Gospel said, panting and pulling up the table leg again.

"He was the same age as your mama, as me. Born just when the worlds were splitting up, if I'm right. He could tell things, just like she could. But he must've *believed*, where she only suspected."

"Suspected what?"

"Don't listen, Merce. Cover your ears," Gospel said.

Auntie just talked over him. "That God was angry. Everything was doomed. Who knows what he believed? He never told your mama." She shook her head and stepped in one slow pace closer. The fumbling hands of the other devil were reaching for the fallen head again, but I couldn't move myself, couldn't react beyond staring at Auntie. "One day, when you were still very young, five years old, maybe," she continued, and now her voice was soft and gentle, like she was telling a story at bedtime, "he took his gun, and he shot himself."

"No." I could feel tears in my eyes, but I couldn't make myself wipe them away.

"It didn't happen that way," Gospel said. "It didn't, Merciful." But he wasn't much of a liar, my brother, and I could tell he was fibbing. "He didn't shoot himself. He died in a fight, with a stranger."

"That's not true," Auntie said, still soft and sweet. "There was no stranger. It's not even a good story, is it? But you believed it because it's what you wanted to believe. If there had been such a person, and he'd killed your father, how did you two and your mother survive? Your mama told you he was protecting you from the stranger, that's how he got killed, but if that's so, then why did the man just leave? No, your papa killed himself when he realized what was coming. The end of the world. And your mama hated his gun after that. And even if Gospel managed to keep the gun, all the bullets were thrown away. I remember it clearly from the dreams I shared with your mama. There aren't any bullets, Merciful."

I was shaking by then, shaking with sorrow and

shock. "He didn't kill himself," I said, but my voice was weak and shuddery. The gun was barely in my grip anymore.

She slowly, sadly nodded her head once, milky eyes fixed on mine. I couldn't look away, couldn't break the spell she had me under. And then Gospel was there between us, the club reeling back, only this time it wasn't no surprise, and Auntie caught the table leg and wrenched it aside, then smacked Gospel down with her other hand. He dropped like a stone, crying out in pain.

"Shoot her, Merce," he gasped out. I raised up the gun again, only I knew it didn't matter.

"Yes. Go ahead and try," Auntie said, stepping onto Gospel as she approached me. He groaned.

"Shoot . . . her."

The crack was as loud as anything I'd ever heard. As loud as the loudest thunder, and as strong. Mama's body lurched back, a thick white fluid oozing from a hole in her chest. The gun had kicked horribly when I pulled the trigger, and my arms were aching, but I had done it. She stumbled back, dropping against the wall just next to the doorway. A sudden motion swept past her. The headless Widow, with something round clutched under one arm, had darted past and into the darkness of the sitting room. I just watched the devil leave, too surprised to even move the gun from where it hung in my hands. Where had the bullet come from?

"There can't be any bullets," Auntie said, her voice now very wet, more of the pale gooey stuff coming out of her mouth. "Your mother got rid of them all."

"I went and found them right after," Gospel said. "Some of them, at least. She tossed them pretty far." He crawled back to me, panting out breaths. "And I loaded up the gun and been carryin' it that way for a while, just in case. Ever since I saw that mist . . . I knew it was trouble. And I was going to be ready, just in case there was something a gun could shoot that might come on out of it. Didn't happen like I expected. Then again, I didn't never think it was Merciful as would pull the trigger." He winced and gasped as he pushed himself to his feet. "We got to find the Minister, Merciful. Maybe it can get rid of this one, now that it's weak."

"You don't want to do that," the thing said, but it wasn't hardly moving now; only the face was still active. Mama's face. I shot my mama. My face crumpled, hot tears burning trails down my cold cheeks.

And then Gospel did something I never thought would happen: he reached out and took hold of me, awkward and loose, like you'd hold a little chick, afraid of crushing it. "Don't you cry, Merce. Don't you cry now, when you done the right thing. You done the right thing, and I'm proud of you."

I wondered if this was really my brother, who I thought hated me but was holding me, all tender, and I just cried more while he told me to hush. He took the gun out of my hand, though he had to pry my fingers loose, and he slipped it back in its holster. When we looked around again, Auntie was gone, which I suppose didn't surprise me much. All that was left was a little puddle of white where she'd rested, and a few drops that showed that she'd quietly slipped past us to the cellar. I guess she didn't want nothing more to do with her "old friend," no more than we did.

"Leastwise we know where she is. Better than that other," Gospel said. "You all right to go on? I figure we got to find the Minister now. There can't be too much time left."

"Yeah. I'm . . . all right." Mostly I just felt tired, tired and empty, like I couldn't cry no more, couldn't get any more upset, and like nothing in the world could shake me. I was wrong, of course, but that's how I felt.

I took up the lamp, and with Gospel in front of me casting a long shadow, we started into the sitting room.

TWENTY~TWO

OUR BREATHS CAME OUT AS BIG CLOUDS OF MIST IN THE
sitting room. After being in the kitchen, where it had
actually been a little warm, it seemed terrible frosty
again. My teeth felt like they were shaking right out of
my head, though maybe that was a little bit because I was
scared. Anything that could pick itself up after what
Gospel did to it and just run off, that was something to
be scared of. I wished I still had the gun in my hands,
even though my arms felt like jelly from having shot it,
and probably would have fallen clean off if I pulled the
trigger again.

I heard a faint noise and realized it was Gospel pulling out his knife, the wicked sharp thing that he carried
for skinning squirrels and suchlike. It made me feel a
little better to know he had it, though I wished it was
bigger. I'd have preferred it if he hadn't been walking
slow and stiff from the hits he took from Auntie, but at

least we had his knife; the gun, too, if we needed it, though I wasn't sure how many more bullets there were.

The light was pretty dim and wavering because I couldn't hold the lamp steady, but I was still looking at the floor for any sign of where the horror that was the Widow had gone to. The floor was all slick with the icy blood, though, so that I couldn't tell anything at all, not even at the bearskin rug, which was clean of mess but didn't have any sign she'd been by neither. Gospel didn't spend any time looking around but pressed forward, with me just behind him. I didn't want to have him leave me. We didn't pause at anything until we came to the door of the bedroom, pushed close but not shut tight. There was light beyond, flickering orange light from the fire in there, which should have been a lot smaller by now but didn't seem to be. Maybe the things had built it up while they had their little chat, though I couldn't see them needing light or warmth or just about anything human.

"You all right to go in, Merce?" Gospel asked. I think he really meant it too, wondering how I was.

"I think so. I can be brave for a little bit longer."

"I don't expect all this will take too much more time, so a little bit should do it," he said, with a grim sort of chuckle. He reached over with his free hand and squeezed my shoulder, then turned away from me.

Gospel stuck out the knife and hooked it inside the

door to give it a pull. The bedroom was lit up by the fire, which was roaring in the hearth, almost all the wood from the pile on it, only one big log a foot around and a foot long left for later. If there was a later. Gospel stepped in, with me still right behind him, and he jumped as he looked around. I did too when my eyes followed his and saw the Widow Cally sitting up in Mama's rocker with her head on her lap, hands crossed dainty on the bald top, rings glittering and shining in the light. The eyes on the head were open, and the mouth, too, open in a broad grin that showed off the Widow's strong, white teeth.

"Come on in and have a seat, children," the head said, with the same mannish voice, though I couldn't think how it was making the sound, not being attached to any lungs or breath at all.

"I don't believe we're going to do that," Gospel said, though we were in the room already. The seat, well, I agreed with him absolutely. I didn't want to sit down near that thing, like it was time for a story by the fire.

"Well, stay standing, then. It's the same to me. I've got things I'm going to tell you, and then you can decide what to do. Stay or go, kill me or not, though I don't know if you can manage it. I'm not as weak as she was, let me tell you. Are you ready to listen?"

"No," Gospel said, but at the same time I said, "Go on." My brother turned back to glare at me, and I cringed from his look. There was nothing this thing had to say that I wanted to hear, nothing at all, only I wanted to know the truth, or try to figure it out. So there was nothing I could do but put out my lip to Gospel's glare and hear whatever filth the thing wanted to spread. "Go on," I said again.

"I was a murderer in the other world. Maybe I will be in this one too, so don't interrupt." The face on the old woman's lap smiled. It gave me the shivers. I reached into Gospel's coat again and dragged out the gun, hoping it was hidden behind my brother. Gospel didn't react, but he must have known what I was doing. "I was given to Rebekkah to do her experiments on. She was trying to find some dream world: a place that wasn't dying. Here, I suppose. Funny—you're dying too, aren't you? Just in a different way.

"But I died there, in my world. They killed me, for my sins as they'd say. And when I died, I finally saw the world she was talking about. I was dead, but I could see it." The shoulders shrugged, but with no head above them it looked just awful.

"I could see this world, and I came to it. And right off, I knew things: I knew that God and the Devil are one and the same, and I knew that He was killing us all. Killing me and my world, and killing you and your world. And damn it if I was going to let that bastard get away with it."

"We should just shoot it, Merciful," Gospel said. I shook my head.

"Don't even try it, girlie. I've killed before. I'd do it again without thinking twice. No, you just listen, because I'm telling you why you should help me. That squirrel thing, that Minister, it's got a straight line to God. I can see it, plain as day. It glows. It shines with a light brighter than the sun. Leastwise it does when I look at it with these here eyes," the deep voice said, lifting the head a little from its lap. "It's 'cause I'm dead, and 'cause I'm not from here. Makes me special."

"Just shoot the damned thing!"

"I'm listening, Gospel. I'm trying to figure out what's really happening."

"Smart girl. Always try to figure out what's going on, who's getting the short end of the stick. That's us, right now. But if we get the Minister, we can turn it around. Through it, I can make God scream out in pain."

"That's not right. We can't . . . you can't hurt *God*. He's God."

"All things are possible, sweetness. For everything there's a season. Even punishing the Creator."

"Do it your damned self," Gospel said.

"I can't. Can't touch the thing, can't get hold of it. It's too strong for me. But not for you."

"We're just kids," I said.

"You're the last people in the world. That's plenty, believe me. Plenty to get hold of that Minister. And then we take some revenge on God."

"But Auntie says we should just kill it," I said, "not

hurt it." I didn't mean to do either, but I wanted to know whatever this monster could tell me. Probably it would lie, but I guessed I was getting pretty good at telling lies from truth by this time.

"Don't listen to her. She killed your mama, you know. Couldn't come over here, couldn't leave our world, unless that happened."

"That don't make any sense," Gospel said.

"She needed a place to come to. Needed a home for herself. That was your mama. So she drove her crazy with her experiments. Then she killed her."

"She really killed Mama?" I hoped Auntie was good and dead down in the cellar. And if not, I'd go and kill her.

"Sure did. That's what all her work was meant for, to study this world from ours so she could escape. Killing your mother, getting herself to this place, was the final step. I saw it all go down, for a couple years. I don't really blame her: you always want to get out of prison, even if your prison is the whole dying world. But we don't need to worry about her anymore. Just about that Minister." The head chuckled a little bit, a sickly laugh that didn't sound like it came from anything human, which I guess Miz Cally wasn't anymore, not really.

"He's lying to hurt you, Merce," Gospel said.

"I know it."

"Rebekkah killed your mama," the devil said. "That's the truth."

I shook my head. "No, she didn't."

"Who the Hell cares? You got a chance to make God pay for what He's done. Driving your mama mad, killing your papa, leaving you two all alone: if God's so strong, so mighty, and so loving, couldn't He have stopped it? Couldn't He have helped you? But no, all you got was that useless little Minister."

"We can't . . . we're not *supposed* to understand God's will," I said.

"That's just another way for Him to avoid the blame, isn't it? I mean, Hell, the guys I killed didn't understand why I did it. Don't mean I had a good reason. Least not as the way they would see it, right?"

I didn't know what to say. There was badness and wickedness in the world, yes, and God let it happen, yes. But I just had to trust that there was a plan, even if I couldn't guess at what it was. Even if maybe it was a bad plan. "I trust God."

"That's helped you a whole lot, hasn't it, girl? Better to trust Him once you've got some leverage. Once the Minister's in your hands and you can make Him sweat."

"Why would we help you with that?" Gospel asked.

" 'Cause it feels good to get back at someone. Didn't it feel great to bash my head off? Didn't it feel great to shoot the other bitch?"

It hadn't, of course. It had felt terrible. Oh, there was a moment, a tiny, tiny moment, when I had been kind of excited and happy just to do something, to save Gospel and defend myself, but I hated what I had to do to make that happen.

"You don't understand them at all," the Minister's calm voice said from the darkness of the sitting room. I wanted to look for it but didn't dare tear my eyes from the Widow. "This world isn't like yours. They're gentle, even Gospel, who's halfway to the Devil."

"I ain't gentle," Gospel said, but he didn't put anything into saying it.

"Children, come away from him."

I stepped out of the bedroom right away, but Gospel stood there a moment longer. I could see from the doorway his hand tight on the knife, his fingers flexing in the gloves, like he wanted to do something but didn't dare, or like he was trying to make up his mind. But he only backed slowly to the door, shutting it behind him and coming out into the sitting room to stand beside me.

"You'll be back," we heard, muffled and terrible, the man's voice from the Widow's dead mouth. "I'll be waiting."

"You give me that gun, Merce. If you ain't gonna shoot at a moment like that, I'll just hold on to it, okay?"

"I can shoot when it's needful."

"Well if that weren't a needful moment, then do you think there's really going to be another?"

I thought for a minute and then realized he might be right, and handed him the pistol. He put it back inside his coat.

The Minister was waiting on the loom, bright black eyes shining in the light of a lamp that rested on the floor beside it. I wondered how it got the light there, with its tiny squirrel paws, but maybe the Minister wasn't holding to one shape very much anymore. Rules were changing, they all said: why not for the made things too?

"He's right about one thing, children. There isn't much time left. I'm sorry for that, at least. I would have liked to see you grow up."

And maybe that was the saddest thing I'd heard yet. The little machine sitting on the loom, and the faint hint of ache in its voice as it mourned for us who weren't even dead yet. I wished to God that we didn't have to die, but I didn't guess He would listen on that particular request.

"What's really happening, Minister? You got to tell us," Gospel said.

"And can we believe anything you say anymore?" I asked.

"I have only been untruthful when it was necessary, and I won't lie to you now." If the Minister could've sighed, it would've, I could tell. But that wasn't something it was made to do, so instead it just dipped its head, rubbing its small paws together. "I will tell you what you need to know. There's no time left anyway, and you should make your choices in knowledge, not ignorance."

"Choices?"

"Hush, Merciful," Gospel said, and the Minister started to speak.

Twenty~Three

"It began with the last war. Such terrors. The slaughter of innocents, and no mercy or pity. God grew angry with man, as He had before. We pleaded for kindness this time, though. We remember the Flood—it was awful. We begged for Him to be gentle and He did as we asked, my brothers and sisters and I. Gentle He was, yes, and kind. But now . . . it's hard to bear, this kindness. Hard to think that everything will soon be nothing."

"Wait just a second, Minister. You spoke to God? Directly?" Gospel said.

"I am His Minister here. Of course I have spoken to Him."

"But you're a made thing, not a . . . I don't know, an angel."

The little nose twitched. "We *were* made, but not here. Long ago, and in a place that you can't understand, God made us. Machines, made things, devices: you had so many names for us when we first came to you."

"I thought all the machines went away after the Last War," I said.

"We were not machines, Merciful. We were the Ministers. You mistook us, as mortals will."

Gospel drew a breath for another question, but I shoved my elbow into his ribs and he shut up. We didn't have the time for his foolishness. Or for mine, if I were honest.

"When God grew angry," the Minister continued, "we asked for mercy, and He in His wisdom granted it. A slow ending, a winding down, and He would start again. There would be less freedom this time, and fewer opportunities to make bad choices, to choose evil. Even in the ending of days, in the twilight of the world, God knew that people would need guidance away from evil, or else the world might end on its own, outside of His plan. That's what free will allows, you understand—it means that God's plan isn't ever final. You, fragile wonderful creatures that you are, can disturb it and rattle it like the windows in this house." They were rattling hard, for the wind was fierce and carried so much snow that they looked white.

"So we were sent, one and all, and I was the first, to this very place, where I saw Esmeralda Cally as a girl, freshly married when I arrived. And years later, both of you would be born. And a hundred, a thousand, a million other Ministers went out into the world, under various names and seemings. And every one with a power about them, to calm people and shape people with words, so that you all became better and better. Even you, Gospel, who imagine you are so very wicked.

"Years passed, and the world changed. There were bad times and bad things, but the people were good." It paused, paused and looked at us for a long while with tiny eyes that seemed happy and sad all at once. "Then the winding down began as we had known it would, whether we made you better or not. Only, if we did it right, all the flocks we had tended would go to Heaven, and if we didn't . . . well, not a one of us liked to think about that, I'll tell you. But for the most part this world died without sin and went to God. The people found their way to Heaven."

"You made us good so we could die?" I asked, with a catch in my throat.

"Everyone dies, Merciful. Every single person who's ever lived was meant to die one day. The best we could hope for, the best *you* could hope for, was Heaven afterward, and the eternal bliss of the presence of God. That's what we tried to give to you, one and all. I think we Ministers did well enough."

I hadn't spent much time thinking about Heaven, truth be told. It had always seemed a long way away, and not much of a patch on Earth. Angels and harps and clouds were one thing, but a life was another, with a man and little ones, a house and a garden plot. That was something I wanted, not Heaven. "Why didn't you just make us better and let us be, then? Let us die naturally in our own time?"

"The world was being wound down, Merciful. This *is* your time. We saved what we could, all that was really valuable. Your souls."

"God damn it, why didn't you save *us*? Why didn't you save Mama or Miz Cally or any of them?" Gospel was real angry, and his hands kept making fists.

"I did save both of them. I brought them to their reward."

"But they died!" I shouted. "They got killed, the both of them, and you didn't do a thing!"

"And I regret the manner of it, Merciful," the Minister said. "I am alone, and my power is almost all tied up in finishing off the world. I could not make an easy end for them. And I cannot for you, either."

"Then what blasted use are you?" Gospel asked, and I felt like saying just about the same thing. What use was a Minister who couldn't protect us, like they said they always would? Who couldn't, or wouldn't, guide us? Why did it even exist?

And then I knew what we had to do, Gospel and I. He was still ranting on while the sad, dark eyes of the Minister looked at us with something like pity, but I put my hand on Gospel's arm and he got quiet.

"We got to go talk to Auntie," I said.

"What for? She's full of lies like the other one."

"But she knows how to stop this."

"She doesn't," the Minister said, but I could tell that it was scared, terrible scared, when it said that.

"Maybe she don't. But we'll go and listen to her anyway. You just told us there ain't much you can do, so what use are you to us? Maybe she's got something instead. I'm sure as heck not ready to die just yet."

The Minister's tale was terrible, but was it worse than the thing in the Widow? Not a bit. Worse than Auntie? I didn't know yet.

"Stay here with me, children, and wait. I can make you comfortable. Make you ready for His embrace."

"Wait?" Gospel said, spitting out the word. "Wait for the end of everything, for the damned fog to come chew us up like it did Jenny Gone? Hell, no. We'll take our chances. We'll make our own choices." I took up the lantern that was sitting near the little made thing, and we started out of the room.

"Be careful of those choices, children. The world's ending is no more set in stone than anything else. It can be worse than this. Much worse." The Minister's warning words followed us out of the room, as I could tell its eyes did, but I made myself not look back. You should never look back. It'll only break your heart.

Twenty~Four

The kitchen still had the touch of warmth what the Minister had left in it, and the fire still burned brightly, but I didn't feel any better for being there. Spatters of blood on the floor, white gunk from where Auntie had got shot, the smell of the gun in the air—I didn't want to be there longer than I needed. But at the same time, I wasn't any too eager to go into the cellar and wouldn't be going at all but for Gospel leading the way. I didn't expect the thing down there to be too happy with me, and I expected it would still be pretty perilous to talk with.

Gospel took a deep breath and stopped in the kitchen, in the middle of all the wreck and ruination. "Merciful. I got to tell you something. Something hard."

"Is it about Papa?" I asked.

He nodded. "Yes. And it ain't a nice story. It's a sad story."

I bit at my lips a second and then let out my breath in

a whoosh. "I reckon I should hear it all the same, shouldn't I?"

"You were just a little girl," he said. "It was a bit before you turned six. You remember? I was playing with you, with those little wooden men I used to have. We were in the bedroom, and you'd made a fort out of the pillows, and my men were attacking yours."

It came back to me clear as day. Gospel wasn't quite nine, and we were still, as best we could be, friends. Even if we argued about our little games. And then . . . I shut my eyes as Gospel kept talking.

"Such a crack. You looked over at me, and I thought maybe you were going to cry. I knew what it was, but I didn't tell you."

"It was the gun. A gunshot."

"You didn't know that, Merce. Not yet. We told you later, but you didn't know it then. I grabbed you down off the bed, and you started to cry because I'd wrecked the game. You still had one of the wooden men in your hand, and you held it real tight to your chest. I pushed you under the bed."

And that I remembered: under the bed, with the dust and an old sock and a folded-up blanket and a pair of shoes that didn't fit anyone quite right, too big for me and too little for Gospel. It was hot and close under there. Outside it was late summer, with the bees buzzing around, and the honeysuckle smell filled the air, but under the bed it was just stuffy.

I could remember that I had lain there and watched Gospel flipping down the blankets, and then I was alone, almost in the dark, and then I started to cry. Quiet, gulping sobs, but nobody came: not Mama or Papa, and not Gospel, who'd left me there.

And then something pushed up under the blanket and came and sat down next to me. In the light when it came in, I could see it was a cat: plump and gray and with yellow eyes that shone under the bed.

"Don't be afraid, Merciful," the Minister had said to me.

"I'm scared, Minister," I said, and reached out and drew it in to me. It was soft and didn't resist, which as a bigger girl I realized had been strange. But all this memory was something I hadn't thought much about: that terrible day when Papa died, so maybe even then I knew it was peculiar to touch the made thing.

And then the little cat, because that's what it looked like just then, said something I'd completely forgotten. "Do you know what helps sometimes when you're afraid?"

"No, Minister."

"Praying. Will you pray with me, Merciful? Just say what I say. 'Our Father, who art in Heaven,'" its soft voice said, and I recited the Lord's Prayer right along with it.

I don't know how long we lay in the dark that day, me and the Minister. Not all the memory came back to me. But we were there enough time that I felt a little better, I knew that much.

"The Minister came and prayed with me," I told Gospel, there in the broken-down kitchen six years later.

He frowned. "It wasn't there when we came back in," he said.

"Maybe not. But it prayed with me."

"Well. That's good, I suppose. It did something of some use. But we could've used it outside. Me and Mama and the Widow and her son, we all clustered round. Or they all did, the grown-ups, and I hovered, but nobody wanted me there. If they hadn't been taking care of Papa, I'm pretty sure they would've sent me away with a fearsome paddling, but . . . well, that thing in Mama told you the truth. There wasn't no stranger. There was only Papa, and a gun."

"Why didn't you ever tell me?"

"Mama said I couldn't tell you. Not ever. She said it wasn't fair, a girl growing up without her papa, and it would've been worse to have you know."

"But you knew. You knew it all." I wasn't yelling, because the Minister and Auntie and the Widow were all so close, but I was doing a whisper that was halfway to a hiss, and boy was I getting mad.

"Do you think I wanted to, Merce? You think I wanted to know our papa killed himself? Hell, no, I didn't. And the last earthly thing I wanted was for you to have to know it too."

My mouth slowly dropped open, my hand raising to cover it. "That's why you went away."

Gospel sighed. "I didn't mean to. Not at first. But I knew you'd bring it up, and I knew if you brought it up enough, I'd tell you. So I ran into the woods, and I stayed far away as long as I could."

"But why didn't you come back more often? Even when Mama got sick? I was taking care of that. You could've come back, you could've told me. I'm strong enough to take it."

He turned his face from me and stepped a few feet away, kicking at a bit of broken wood. "Oh, Merce. I could've, sure. But by then . . . by then I kind of hated you. Because you didn't have to know. You got to be innocent still and think your papa protected you. And there I was freezing to death in the woods, without a soul to speak to, and with that secret burning a hole in my heart. No, I wasn't going to come back at all. But then the damned fog showed up, and I didn't have no place I could go any further."

I took a step toward him through the broken wood. My hand lifted up, but I didn't quite touch his back. I couldn't imagine what it had been like to hold in a secret like that.

"Do you remember when we came to get you? When Mama and I came back into the house? You were under the bed, and you were playing with that little wooden man there, telling it crazy stories."

"I don't remember," I said.

"Mama told you Papa'd been shot. You started to cry,

and you kicked and hit her and told her she was lying. You said you wanted to see him, if he was dead, and when we wouldn't let you, you said we were both lying: that Papa was alive and we were just keeping you away from him. And Mama just held you close, lying on the bed. I was on mine, under a blanket, peeking out. I was crying so hard, but so quiet. I hadn't said a word since we came in: I didn't trust myself to tell the lie, not yet. And then Mama started to sing."

My skin popped up in goose flesh. "What did she sing?"

"You know," he said. "That song. *'Hush, little baby, don't you cry, Mama's gonna sing you a lullaby.'*" Gospel's voice was rough and awkward, but he sang the words as best he could. "Good Lord, I hated that song ever since, that lying, cheating song. But you stopped crying eventually, and you fell asleep."

"Papa was gone in the morning," I said, remembering.

"The Callys took care of burying him. And we went to see the grave, and you were crying. So she sang that damn song again," Gospel said.

I froze as a noise came from the cellar. *"Hush, little baby, don't you cry, Mama's gonna tell you why you'll die."* The horrible voice so close to Mama's but not quite, a little gurgly and wet and very faint, was singing again as we came to the open cellar door. Gospel looked back at me, a touch nervous, I supposed, and I sure as Heaven was feeling the same. He licked his lips, and his fist got tight on his knife.

"Are you ready to talk to her?" he asked.

I didn't trust my voice to speak, so I only nodded. But I reached out and took his hand for a moment, and I pressed it hard. He tried to smile, with his black-blistered nose and cheeks and his bruised face, and then he started down the steps.

If I hadn't been holding his hand, I don't know if I could've followed. But I didn't have any choice. Down into the dark we went, with my mama's old song of comfort twisting in the air around us.

TWENTY~FIVE

THE STAIRS CREAKED UNDER GOSPEL'S FEET, AND THE
voice fell suddenly silent. Halfway down, I slipped on
frost that was thick on the lowest steps. I caught myself
on a frigid wall. "Lord, it's cold down here," I said, my
breath misting up.

"Shouldn't be this cold," Gospel said, helping me
back up.

"I don't like it."

"Let's go quick, before it gets any worse." We went
real careful down the last few stairs, and I held the lamp
up high at the bottom. Resting next to the pile of wood,
barely visible in the flickering light, was Mama's body.

There was a pool of something white around it, that
same stuff that had poured out of the hole in her chest
where I shot her. It wasn't frozen, and it must've been
pretty warm still because it was giving off steam, or perhaps that was just how cold it'd got. Mama's head turned

up to look at us, the eyes bloody and white at the same time, milked over but with angry red lines all through.

"I was wondering if you'd get here in time," she said, sounding almost like Mama.

"In time for what?" I asked, though I knew the answer.

"Before I go, of course," she said, and it made me shiver because Mama *had* gone, only two or three days ago. I'd lost track. I wished that I'd had a chance to talk to her like I was about to talk to Auntie, but Mama's end came on too sudden. "I don't think I'll last much longer." A horrid wet chuckle came out of her. "I came to your world because I thought it would be a way to keep living. And here I am, still dying."

"You're really dying?"

"Oh, yes. All over again. I was dying in my world too, dying of cancer and weariness and boredom. It sounds so banal now. Cancer, that's something people die of. But weariness? Boredom? How ridiculous."

"What's cancer?" Gospel asked.

"It's an old disease people used to get," I answered, because I had read it in one of the books Mama had on her shelves, on one of the long nights when I watched over her while Gospel was off somewhere being the Devil's creature.

"No cancer here, even? Well . . . a doomed bit of paradise. Or maybe we got the worst of it, where I'm from. Two worlds: this one where the souls were being saved, a place for the good girl. That one, mine, like a twisted reflection, an accident. The horrible brother who hunts in the woods."

"Hey!" Gospel said, but she just talked over him: "The mad mother who screams at things she can't see. Every terrible thing that wasn't here, though, we got. War and hatred, too many people and too much disease, aches and misery and horror. You talk about the Last War. We had it too. My father fought in it, before I was born."

"Mama's father did too," I said.

"Of course he did. They were the same person. Until a few years after the Last War, we were all the same people. Until just about when I was born—when your mama was born. Then it all changed."

"God changed it," Gospel said, right as I was thinking the same.

"Yes. Only I don't believe in God. Even now, I don't believe in God, and I should. I really should." Other than her lips, I realized she hadn't moved at all since she tilted up her head. The eyes hadn't blinked, there hadn't been a twitch of the hands, nothing at all. "When I first started dreaming of your mama, I thought I was mad. But the dreams were so real. I didn't do anything about it for a very long time, but eventually I entered into sleep studies, went to labs . . . oh, you don't understand me. You can't. There's nothing like that left here, and hasn't been for years, I'm sure."

"I know what a lab is," I said, and Gospel said he did too, though I didn't believe he knew any such thing.

"Not the sort I mean, I'm sure, but good enough. The doctors couldn't figure out how I had these dreams, how I knew things I shouldn't. I think it's because your mama and me were born so close to when things changed. We were, more than most, the same person. I found a way to contact your mama, from my dreams to hers. But not well, not often, not reliably. And I don't think she ever really understood what was happening."

"You made her go crazy," I said, remembering all the times Mama had talked to something that wasn't there, had gotten mad and angry and frustrated at things she couldn't control. And I remembered what the thing up in the rocker had said too, that this Rebekkah had done it, made my mama mad.

"I never intended that." She paused after she said it, paused for long enough that I wondered if she had expired. "I just wanted to know what was happening to me. And then the world—my world—went out of control. The air was poison, the land was dying, disease was everywhere. But even with all that, hardly a single person cared. We just didn't mind a thing but ourselves any longer. I wasn't much different. I sank into my work with your mama and let the rest of the world pass me by."

"You should've helped," I said, because I couldn't stand her talking about how selfish she was anymore. "Your world needed you."

"You don't understand. It wasn't just me. *Nobody* cared. None of us did anything. It's all over now. We faded away to nearly nothing. Shallow and meaningless. And I was dying anyway, and then there was a way to try to fix things, I thought, to come here when your mama died."

"But you were the one who killed her. The other thing told us," Gospel said, real hate in his voice for a moment. I got a grip on his shoulders, at the frosty bottom of the steps, but he didn't make to move forward.

"Did James tell you that? It's not true. Did he tell you he was a murderer, and that he was about to die for it when I saw him last? I don't know that I'd trust him."

"He told us about dying, that he was killed as punishment for doing bad things."

"Well. More truth than I thought he had in him. But I didn't kill your mama. Not really. I probably didn't help her live any longer, but I didn't kill her. I think maybe she got some of my apathy, the same way I got some of her madness. And one day she just gave up, gave up and died."

"Mama wouldn't do that," I said, but I didn't really believe it. I never thought there'd be so many secrets, so many lies, in my little family, but there were, and I didn't think I could ever know the truth of it anymore. I had to try, though. It mattered, the truth; even if the world was ending, the truth still had to mean something.

"Maybe not. But that's what it seemed like to me. I

woke up from a dream in a sweat, tired and aching, and I knew she was dead. I just knew. So I went to my machines, and I went back to sleep with them running, and I dreamed of her, only she was gone. I managed to cross the bridge. I came here, into her, by bits and pieces. It was like a door had been left open for me, and I could creep in when I slept. In my dreams, I saw you, I spoke with you. And then . . . then *I* died, and at last I arrived."

"But why'd you come here?"

"To kill the Minister. Just as I said." She coughed, white fluid spitting out of her mouth. The puddle around her was bigger, still steaming in the wintry air. "The Minister was the means by which God split the worlds, it and all the other Ministers, though the rest were just helpers to this one, and all of them are gone now. If we kill the Minister, I believe everything will be undone. The first shall be the last. It's the alpha and the omega." Talk from the Good Book, that was, but Auntie didn't even believe in the Lord.

"How can you kill it?" Gospel said.

"I can't. But *you* can. As easy as using your knife. Your hands. Anything."

"What'll happen?" I asked, my voice barely more than a whisper.

"I don't know what it'll mean, I don't know what world will be made, but it's got to be better than the one I lived in and died in. And it's got to be better than this place, with the world falling in around us and about to stop altogether. Doesn't it have to be better?"

I thought about Jenny Gone being eaten by the nothing of the fog. I thought about wanting to grow up and about meeting a boy. I never would now, even if the fog just stopped, which I didn't expect could happen. I thought about how I was going to die before I was a day older.

"Yeah," Gospel said, his voice firm. "It would have to be better than this damned place. It would."

I didn't want to, but I nodded. I couldn't think of anything worse than our present situation, dying cold and lonely in a hard place like this. And, oh, how I hated that maybe she was right, horrible creature that she was. But, after all, it was why we had come down: to try to find out what we might do.

"Good. I think it's too late for me, in the new world you'll make, but maybe not. Maybe your mama and I will get another chance.

"Go now. Go and find the Minister. I don't think it can stop you except with words. I don't think it can ever hurt humans." The voice was growing weaker, quieter, like now that she'd said her piece she was done with talking.

"It almost killed Miz Cally," I said.

"She wouldn't have died. The Minister was protecting its secret. That's spoiled now. Too late in the game for it to even be able to do that much. I think all the strength it has is taken up in closing down the world."

"It might run away again." I kind of hoped it would, even though I didn't want to die. I just didn't think I wanted to kill the Minister either.

"Not far. Not now. It has to be in the center when the world ends, I'm betting."

The Minister had kept talking about how it couldn't get close to the fog, and now the fog was closing in. She was right. It couldn't run very far. "This house is the center?"

Her voice was so quiet, I could barely hear her at all now. "The last place on Earth I would expect to be the last place on Earth. But there it is. And here we all are. And you two have a task to see to. Go on, and come see me when it's over, if you can. I'll try to hold on. Or maybe I'll come see you, huh?" Her head dropped down to her chest. I thought for a minute she was dead, but then I heard, faint and seeming far away, that same old song again.

"*Hush, little baby, . . . don't . . . you . . . cry. . . .*" But I did, I started crying for Mama, who was dead, and for Auntie, who had just wanted to live, and for myself, who wanted to live but was going to be dead anyway. For everybody else too, I was crying. The tears were cold on my cheeks right after I shed them.

"Come on, Merciful. Let's go. We got a job to do," my brother said, just like he was aiming to set up a fence or beat the rugs. That was Gospel, though. I don't think he cared none for any of it, just wanted to have it done.

Only I saw tears on his cheeks too as he went past me real fast, his feet banging on the stairs.

I looked for what I figured would be the last time at Auntie sitting there, singing out from the wreck of Mama's body, and tried without much success to pretend that when I went up those stairs it wasn't Mama I was leaving there too. And then I climbed up the steps, into the warm kitchen, and went to go kill the Minister.

Twenty~Six

"ARE YOU OKAY?" MY BROTHER ASKED ME WHEN WE were both at the top of the steps. "That was a bitter thing, to have to see Mama like that again. I'm sorry we had to do it."

"It's nearly all bitter now. But it's almost over, right?"

He nodded. "Almost."

There was light in the sitting room, a faint blue glow that reminded me of the full moon. I held Gospel back as we circled the wreck of the kitchen table, held him back because I didn't know what we might see in there. There wasn't a thing in the house that shone blue like that. "What do you think that is?" I whispered to him.

"Hell if I know, Merce. Hell if I can even guess." He sounded so tired, so worn, and I wondered if he was well at all, or how bad he was still hurting from the beating he got earlier and from the frostbite that still marked his face.

"Well, we got to end it the right way."

"Don't you or me know what's right anymore, so don't pretend you do. We're just doing what seems best, minute to minute. And like you just said, we ain't got much more time to get confused. Now, are we going in there, or are we staying in here?"

"In there," I said, and gave him a little push. He started forward, my brother with his knife held out before him, and I followed careful and cautious, falling a little behind, because Gospel being Gospel, he was moving fast for trouble. He got into the room and stopped right there, staring over to the left at where we'd left the Minister. When I peeked in around him, I could see what had stopped him, and it stopped me, too.

The Minister was still the Minister, a little gray squirrel sitting on the lower lip of the loom, with tiny wet black eyes and furry small-clawed paws. It was looking at us, not seeming to have moved much at all since we'd left it. And yet . . . there was something more there. There was a shape around it, a shape that passed through the loom, or into the loom, or something that my eyes couldn't rightly describe to me. A tall man, maybe, though you could see right through it and there wasn't much more than the idea of a man. And it was shining, that manshape, shining with a faint blue light that lit up the room, and warmth was coming off of it.

Or maybe it just looked like an angel now—maybe it *was* an angel, to be able to talk to God and be at the Flood and who knew what all else—and everyone knew angels glowed, leastways they did in the Good Book, in the pictures.

"I don't like the looks behind your eyes," the Minister said. It reared up onto its haunches. The man shape around it didn't move at all.

"What do you mean, Minister?" Gospel said, trying to sound innocent. He'd always been bad at that trick.

"The way you hold that knife, the way you walk, everything suggests to me that you have made a decision. A bad one, if I'm any judge of right and wrong. One that shows you're halfway to the Devil." Which he was, it didn't say, but we both knew.

Gospel stepped forward, circling around the back of Papa's chair toward the loom, behind Mama's. The Minister watched him come closer. I stepped over the threshold into the room and felt so much warmer, felt warmth shining out from the Minister, from the glowing image of what I now thought of as an angel.

"I heard you talking with the thing in the cellar," the Minister said. "I heard it, and I heard you, and I know what you mean to do. You should be ashamed," it said. But Gospel, he wasn't a strong one for shame, and so he kept on walking.

I heard the creak of the rocker and horrible thumps, the dreadful clumping thumps of hard footsteps on the floor, coming rapid and loud, and then the thing that had been the Widow was at the door. The head was in its right hand, and something bulky was in the left. It pulled back that hand, holding the head high with the right, and I called out, "Gospel, *duck!*" but my stupid brother didn't hardly listen. He turned a bit and cringed down, and the Minister bounced to the side on the frame, and then that last log from by the fire flew across the room and slammed into Gospel's chest. The knife dropped from his hand as he flopped into the corner of the room, bouncing off the linen chest and landing with a ragged crash on the ground. I swore I heard a bone snap in the hit.

The Minister, what had bounded aside to avoid the log entire, sprang off the frame with the faint blue shape around him still and landed right next to Gospel, reared up and fierce, its tail puffed out.

"Capture it, Merciful," the thing in the Widow said. James, that was its name. "Get it. We'll make God pay for what He's done."

"What you done, more like," I said. I ran over to Gospel and dropped on my knees beside him. The thing in the door didn't move, only stood there with the head lifted up high to crane a view over the chairs. "Is he alive?" I asked the Minister.

"For the moment, yes. He is . . . very badly hurt." The little creature didn't look over at Gospel, just kept its eyes trained on the staring head. The Widow monster hadn't moved closer, just shifted from side to side.

I checked my brother over, careful not to touch him too rough. His chest felt wrong, kind of soft, and there was blood on his lips, and bubbles that formed up when he breathed in and out. But at least he was still breathing.

"He can't dare touch you now," the Minister said, very softly. "You're his last chance. He needs a mortal to touch me, to destroy me."

"What do you mean?"

"He's an abomination. He's not really part of God's creation. So creation doesn't respond to his will any longer, not like it responds to yours." I didn't understand exactly what it meant. I just stared down at Gospel and shook my head. "You're the last one who can make any decisions," the Minister insisted, "the last one whose free will matters. You can stop that thing."

"Or you can capture the Minister. Kill it, if you like," the man's voice said from the dangling head of the old woman. "I can hear you, you know. There isn't too much other noise now."

And there wasn't, I realized. The wind, the hiss of the snow, it had all stopped sometime in the last few minutes.

"Why's it so quiet?"

"The world is very small now, Merciful. There's not enough of it left for the wind to blow, for the snow to rustle. There might not be snow falling anymore, in fact. The fog's cut off even the lowest of the clouds."

"How long do we have?"

"Half an hour, maybe. A little more or less, if you struggle against it or if you accept it. The choice is yours, as it was always going to be."

I had half an hour to live, or to die. I had half of one hour, that was all, to decide what if anything I was going to do. Gospel couldn't help me and the Minister wouldn't help me and no one else was left. I wanted to cry again, but I'd cried about all I could. I'd cried for good reasons and bad, and I was going to try my hardest not to waste time doing it again.

"Take it, Merciful," the devil said. "Take the Minister and hold it, and I'll show you what to do."

I looked at the little squirrel, standing so brave in front of Gospel, and I knew that I wouldn't take it and hold it. I knew that no matter what I did, I wouldn't let the little thing be tortured or whatever it was that the monster wanted to do. The light around the Minister, the glowing shape like a man, was getting brighter, and I could see outlines—a face that was handsome and gentle, and strong arms, and a faint shimmering of broad wings. I knew that it was an angel, just like it had said. I knew it, and I knew I could never let that kind of hurt be done to it.

The needful moment had come, I guessed.

I reached inside Gospel's jacket. His chest felt weak and soft, and I tried not to notice that as I took hold of the gun, warm from being against his body. I'd only shot it off the one time, but it already felt cozy in my hand, like it sort of belonged there. I stood up, with the gun tugging my tired arms down.

"What's your name?" I asked.

"Gabriel," the Minister said.

"Not you." I hadn't even thought it would have a name. "That one." I knew what Auntie had called it, but I wanted to know if she was lying, wanted to know if I could trust anything she had said, and this was the only card I had left to play.

"I have no name any longer."

"You do," I said. I took a single step and raised up the gun. "Tell me your name."

"You can't kill me. I'm not as weak as that thing below. My hate makes me strong." Its voice was dark and evil when it spoke, and I got a shiver up my back because I knew it was terrible still. But I had listened when the Minister had talked, and I had figured things out. I knew something.

"Fine. Don't have a name. Makes it easier to say good-bye." And I pulled the trigger. The shot went far wide, no chance I had hit anything, but the monster was surprised as all get-out anyway, and it bolted back into the bedroom.

"Don't you let Gospel die, Minister. Gabriel. Don't you dare," I said, and I went after the thing in the Widow. There wasn't a good place to hide in the bedroom, and anyway the Widow had been too big to just go about hiding. But it wasn't hiding. It was standing right by the fire. The head was back in place atop that long body, and in the shadowy light it almost looked to be Miz Cally, from her nearly bald crown down to her booted feet, one ringed hand shining in front of her mouth as if she'd been caught in a gasp.

"Don't shoot, Merciful," she said, and it was the Widow's voice, just the same as when she was calling on the Good Lord against the thing in the cellar. "I'm still here. I'm still inside."

And I stopped in my tracks, because I didn't know. Maybe somehow she was still in there. Maybe the Widow had been fighting to get out all this time, and now the thing was so terrible afraid that she was winning. Only . . . even if she had been there before, Gospel had knocked the body so hard, she'd be dead now. She had to be dead now. Dead, and I hoped she was with God in His Heaven just like the Minister had said. I raised up the gun and stepped closer, so that I was just out of the thing's long reach, barely back out of danger.

"You can't kill me," the thing said in its man voice. "You can't kill what's already dead."

And maybe I couldn't. But I'd try anyway. The rules were changing. I screwed up my face.

"My name is James," the thing said suddenly. I wondered if it thought that would stop me, thinking it was a person with a name like anyone else. But it wouldn't. It just proved what Auntie had told me, proved that he was a killer and a terror and worse than anything else in all this narrow world. He was wicked through and through, and there wasn't no point to leaving him be just because once, long ago, his mother had named him James.

"That's a nice name. But I don't suppose I care about that anymore," I said, and I pulled the trigger again. The gun bucked in my hand and smoke jumped up in front of me and the thing staggered back and into the fireplace. I didn't stay to look at it, didn't want to know if it was dead or alive, didn't want to do anything more. I stumbled back out of the room, closing the door behind me.

"You killed it?"

I dropped the gun and shrugged, spent. "Maybe. I don't know. It fell over." Into the fire, I didn't say, but I started to pray for poor Widow Cally, for Esmeralda, who was my mama's friend and taught me to jump rope. I asked God to please look after her and to please see that she got her time in Heaven, because she was one of the best of souls. And I expected that He heard me when I prayed just then, because I was like as not the only thing in all the world doing any praying. Unless maybe Gabriel was doing some, but I thought it probably didn't really need to pray at all.

"Now just the one in the cellar," the Minister said.

"She's already done for." I walked around to where it rested, the shining shape all around it, and Gospel just behind, with the blood on his lips barely bubbling from tiny, weak breaths. "He's dying, isn't he?"

The little face turned to Gospel. "Yes. He'll probably not make it to the end. But he'll live forever in Heaven."

"Maybe he wanted to live a little longer here," I said, but I knew it was pointless to go wishing. I knelt down beside my brother, empty of tears.

"You'll be back together with him soon enough." The Minister's voice was full of sympathy, but all I could remember was Jenny's missing arm, and I knew that would be the way for me. Quick or not, that would be the way at the end, and I couldn't think of it as a good thing, even with Heaven on the other side.

The light from the Minister was getting real strong, and I could see the shine of the blood on Gospel's lips, could see how his cheeks were starting to peel where the black dead skin was, could see that he was bruised on his chin from I didn't know what. I reached out and took his hand. He might've pushed me away if he could, but there wasn't any strength in his hand. It was limp and weak and didn't do nothing but sit in my sweaty palm.

"Tell me when he dies, Minister."

"You shouldn't think about that, Merciful. You should pray. There isn't much time."

I could smell something on the air, sickly sweet and smoky, and I knew the Widow's body was burning in the bedroom fireplace.

"Tell me when it happens."

It didn't say anything more, just sat there as the light got brighter and the shape around it became more and more what it was: an angel. And then it bowed its little head and didn't say anything, but I knew. I reached up and wiped at Gospel's lips with my sleeve, wiped off the blood as best I could, and leaned in and kissed him on his forehead, then lifted myself back up to my knees.

"So he's in Heaven now?"

The little head bobbed.

"And the Widow? Jenny? My mama?"

"God's love extends to everyone."

"Then why'd He end it all?"

"He was angry." The Minister didn't sound angry itself, only sad.

"That's a stupid reason to kill everything in the world."

I thought I saw the angel wings flutter, as if it were shrugging, but the Minister remained still. "Perhaps. But we can't ever understand God fully." And in its voice I heard that even this being, even an angel, didn't understand. And if even an angel didn't understand, maybe there wasn't anything to understand at all. Maybe it was just stupidity and hurt pride and whatever else God must've felt when the world went a way He didn't want it to. I had to believe, though, that there was something more, that maybe Auntie had told true: I could hope to have faith enough to make it better. I could change the world. The Minister'd said as much itself. But it was a thin hope, and my proof thinner still.

"Come here, Minister," I said, holding out my hands.

It paused only a moment, a moment when I saw the shining arms of light strain just a little, as if they wanted to do something, but it came. It came and looked up at me with soft black specks of eyes, and twitched, and hopped into my hands. It was trembling.

After all the terrible choices we'd made, all us Truths, I didn't know if I was about to make a good one. But I still had a choice, and that was something. I couldn't bear to hurt the Minister, I knew that. But I could kill it, kill it quick and painless. I'd wrung the necks of squirrels before, and in the end the Minister, for all the shining light of Heaven and all the wisdom of ages and all that sort of thing, the Minister wasn't much different. My hands shifted. The little eyes didn't leave mine. And then, just a tiny snap, quieter than a heart breaking.

It got very dark in the sitting room. I could see only shadows. For a moment, I couldn't hear anything at all, and I thought maybe the world had ended when I did what I did. Everything had gotten so quiet, like the hour before dawn, when sometimes Mama would sleep and I might go out on the porch in the still, gray light. I didn't even know if there was a porch outside anymore. In the kitchen, the last wood in the stove gave out a pop. Where I sat, the cold crept back up and curled around me, and I shivered, body and soul at once.

TWENTY~SEVEN

I WAS THE ONLY ONE LEFT, THE ONLY PERSON IN ALL of creation. God's whole concern on Earth now, that was me.

I pushed myself up from beside Gospel and walked in the dim light to the kitchen. There was still a fire there, still burning bright and trying to be warm, though whatever the Minister had done to make the room cozy earlier, it was gone now. I gathered up some of the broken bits of the table and the cabinets, all the things the monsters had smashed, and I carried the wood armload by armload into the sitting room, making a little stack just next to the loom.

When I was gathering up the last load, I heard the cellar stairs creak, but not sounding the way they usually did, and that's when I noticed it. The air at the top of the stairs was fuzzy, misty, the flipped-up hatch fading away. The edges of the boards there didn't connect to the wall any longer, but to nothing at all, just the empty mists that were closing down the world. I wondered if this was how far they had come and now they would stop, or if they were still moving in, even without the Minister. It didn't matter either way. Not anymore.

There was a big, deep pot that we used to boil up preserves in, and I got that, too. It was so big, I could barely carry it with my arms wrapped around it, and so heavy I struggled to move. My foot slipped on something, and I dropped the clumsy thing. I looked down and saw the top part of the little ballerina from the music box, the head and one arm.

I bent over and picked it up. It was chipped and cracked and barely held together.

"*Hush, . . . little . . .*" I whirled around. Auntie was there, or what was left of her, dragging herself up the stairs with cracked and broken hands. She looked thin and frail, like she had been dissolving into the white stuff that smeared her. Her face sagged worse than ever, and I couldn't even see my mama in it anymore. This was just Auntie, now. Her head was tipped down so I couldn't see her eyes, but I thought, in the wavering firelight, that her jaw was moving. The song had got awful quiet if she was still singing, because even in the silence, I couldn't hear a thing.

"You're dead," I said to her. "Dead and gone."

"Did you kill it?"

Soft as a whisper, those words, but I could see that she was really trying hard to speak. Her chin, resting on the top step, had juggled her head around as she moved it, but only the tiniest of sounds came out.

"Yeah. Yeah, I killed it."

"Did everything get better?" I hadn't expected it, but there was hope in the voice, faint and weak as it sounded. After all of this, she still hoped.

"No. It didn't." But I still thought maybe it would. I still hoped, too. The world was almost over, and I didn't have much of a thing to pin my hopes on, but still they were there.

She moaned. "It was supposed to get better. God's cheating."

"You don't believe in God," I said. I looked down at the little ballerina in my hands. I set it down carefully in the pot.

"No," she said. Even though I was so terribly close to her, I couldn't hear her any better. She was fading away.

"I have to ask you this. And you have to answer. You just have to." Nothing, no sound at all. I might have been too late. "Did you kill my mama?"

There was a silence of moments. I stood shaking in the chilly air, wondering why the fire right behind me couldn't make me warm. I needed to know this answer, of all the answers I'd got and not got in the last days.

"I didn't help her," Auntie said. "She was lost and alone, and I did nothing to help her. I was waiting, waiting for her to die. I could've helped her, I think." I had leaned in while she talked, the candle lighting up her horrible face, just so that I could hear her at all.

"But did you kill her? The other one, he said you did."

"I don't think so. I just wanted her to die, wanted to be here, not there. It's stupid now."

She hadn't killed Mama. Hadn't done anything to help but hadn't hurt her. Maybe Auntie had made Mama plumb crazy, but it went both ways, near as I could tell. And it was the end of days. I didn't have it in me to hurt anyone else, to do anything worse than I'd already done. Not for no reason.

The edge of the fog had come closer, was brushing on her far arm. Her legs might already have been gone down below. "I'm going now," I said.

"No. Don't leave me alone."

"I'm sorry. But we're both all alone now."

"You got Gospel."

My eyes went wet again, but I brushed away the tears. "No . . . he . . . he didn't make it."

"Oh, Merciful." At least I think that's what she said. Her voice was less than the step of a cat, than the drop of a snowflake. Maybe I heard it. Maybe I didn't. The edge of nothing slipped over her shoulder. I couldn't watch it happen.

I took up that big kettle, and I struggled and strained and carried it into the sitting room. The ballerina came out, and the smashed-up wood went in, and I lit a fire there, a little thing next to Gospel, who was still and quiet and peaceful, and let it burn in the kettle, with another armload of wood to feed it. I didn't suppose I'd need much more. I set the little bit of the dancer next to Gospel's head and patted it and wished things had been different. And then I took Gospel's hand in mine, and I took a deep breath, and I started to pray.

Not a real prayer, not some kind of Minister-speak. Just talking to the Good Lord and hoping, seeing as I was the last little girl on Earth, that He'd listen. I don't know what all I said, because with the cold and tiredness and all the troubles, I wasn't thinking too straight anymore. I know I asked Him to make things right. I know that I asked Him why everyone had to die. I know I promised that if He gave us another chance, we'd all be better. I didn't think I was lying, because I was the only person who could promise anything right then, and there wasn't anything anyone could say or do to make me into a liar. Not at present, at least.

I told Him all kinds of stupid things, like about the time that I'd hidden a raccoon kit in Gospel's bed but hadn't ever been caught, or the time I ate the last piece of cherry pie and blamed it on my brother, or about how, now and again, I'd been mean to Mama when she wasn't herself and couldn't know. That last part was hard to admit, hard to tell, but I thought I'd better come clean.

I don't know how long I talked, only my throat got

dry, and I could see that the firelight was growing dim and that it was shining on the edge of the mist that had come all the way into the sitting room by that time. And I was still holding Gospel's hand, which was getting cold in mine. He never liked for me to touch him, but I couldn't see it mattering now. His face was white with frost, and I wondered if I had frostbite on my cheeks like he did, because I couldn't feel anything. My lips were shaking, and my teeth were chattering, but I could still talk a little. I could still manage one more prayer.

"The Lord is my shepherd; I shall not want. He makes me lie down in green pastures; He leads me beside still waters. He restores my soul; He guides me in the paths of righteousness for His name's sake. Yea, though I walk through the valley of the shadow of death"—and here my breath caught, and my hand clenched Gospel's, and I didn't know if I could go on—"I shall fear no evil, for Thou art with me; Your rod and Your staff, they comfort me. You prepare a table before me in the presence of my enemies. You anoint my head with oil; my cup overflows." I was sobbing as I spoke, tears freezing on my cheeks in the horrid cold. "Surely goodness and love shall follow me all the days of my life, and I shall dwell in the house of the Lord forever and ever.'" I thought I couldn't have felt a prayer more than when Jenny died, but I was wrong, because I felt this all the way to the bottom of my soul.

I took a deep breath. I only had hope, hope that the

Good Lord would hear me, that what the Minister half told me mattered, that if I wanted hard enough to live, somehow the world would get better. The fog was all around me now, only the kettle and Gospel and the tiny body of the Minister were still inside it. The world was over.

I closed my eyes and silently asked for forgiveness. And then I said the last word in all the world, maybe. The last thing anyone would ever say, to men or angels or God. The last word of the last prayer.

"Amen."

Acknowledgments

A million thanks to my ever-supportive University Book Store crew: Caitlin, Lauren, Kitri, Jamie, Kelsey, Anna, and a clutch of other people who read, commented on, and/or were generally positive about the long process of getting a book from rough draft to publication.

Thanks also to my friend Elana for pushing me to go to the consultation that led me to my wonderful editor, Noa Wheeler. I never would have done it on my own.

Thank you, Noa, for reading and loving the book enough to champion it and make it happen.

And a mass of gratitude to all the rest who have been invaluable to me through the entire process: Nancy Pearl, Brad, Terri, my entire family, Victoria and Bernadette, and always, always, Adam.